Killer Art in the Park

Paula Darnell

Campbell and Rogers Press

ISBN: 978-1-887402-38-5

Cover design by Molly Burton with Cozy Cover Designs

First Edition

Published by Campbell and Rogers Press

https://www.campbellandrogerspress.com

Dedicated, with appreciation,
to all animal lovers who have given a pet
a loving, forever home

Chapter 1

The rocket's red glare started the fight.

Or, more accurately, the fact that Rich, our Fourth-of-July party host, decided to shoot fireworks over his next-door neighbor's house kicked off an argument with him, which quickly escalated to fisticuffs.

When I saw a tall man vault over the five-foot wall between the two properties, I knew trouble was brewing.

"You fool!" the enraged man shouted at Rich. "What do you think you're doing?"

Without waiting for an answer, he rushed forward and took a wild swing at Rich, who didn't back off. Instead, our host threw an equally ineffective punch toward his neighbor, who responded by charging Rich and giving him a forceful shove. Rich staggered backwards but managed to stay on his feet. Balling up his hand into a fist, he came back at his opponent and started to take a swing, just as his brother-in-law Nate grabbed him from behind while Dave, my friend Dawn's husband who just happened to be a police sergeant, held back the neighbor.

By this time, the attention of all the partygoers was on the two red-faced men. Both of them were big guys, so it was a good thing neither had been successful, or somebody could have been badly injured. As it was, they huffed and puffed, scowling at each other.

"If you two don't knock it off, you'll be spending the rest of the night in the county lock-up," Dave declared. "And Rich, your neighbor's right about the fireworks. You shouldn't be shooting any into the air at all. That's not legal in Arizona, as I'm sure you know."

The tall man snickered, but Dave wasn't through yet.

"You're not off the hook, either. I saw you take the first swing. Now let's be reasonable, gentlemen. Rich, I'm going to overlook the fireworks violation this time as long as you stop and apologize to your neighbor here."

"Sorry," Rich mumbled, although it was obvious to me that he wasn't sorry at all.

"And you. What's your name?"

"Hal. Hal Quinlin."

"Same goes for you, Hal. There are better ways to settle a dispute than a fist fight; don't you agree?"

"You're right, officer. I was out of line."

"All right, then."

Rich's wife Pamela, the director of the Roadrunner Art Gallery who'd invited all us member artists to the party, joined them and added, "Hal, we're so sorry. I guess we got caught up in the festivities. Please, we'd love for you to join us, wouldn't we, Rich?"

"Yeah, sure," Rich muttered.

Pamela took Hal's arm and guided him toward the patio where a long table, laden with food, beckoned.

"Please help yourself," she urged. "I'll have Nate put some more hamburgers on the grill."

"OK, make mine medium rare," he said as he took a plate and helped himself to some potato salad and baked beans.

"How about a margarita?"

"Don't mind if I do."

Pamela left him standing next to the grill while Nate flipped hamburgers. Rich had set up a bar in one corner of the patio, so he could serve drinks without having to go into the kitchen for supplies. He glowered as he prepared the margarita and handed it to Pamela, knowing its destination. Although Hal may have settled down, Rich was evidently still seething from the incident.

Brian, my boyfriend, who was also my next-door neighbor, lightly touched my elbow and grinned. "It's always fun to watch fireworks on the Fourth of July," he whispered, "but I had no idea they'd erupt in the middle of the party."

"Very funny. I'm sure poor Pamela is mortified. I'll bet you she didn't know Rich was planning to shoot off those rockets."

"Looks like the excitement's over," Brian said, nodding toward Hal, who'd settled in a lawn chair next to the pool with his hamburgers and margarita.

"And now the real fireworks begin," I said as I pointed toward the sky.

We had a perfect view of the city's annual fireworks display from Pamela's backyard. Although the downtown area was on low ground, the outskirts of Lonesome Valley extended into the foothills of the surrounding mountains. Since that's where Pamela and Rich lived, we enjoyed a great vantage point for watching the dazzling display, which was launched from one of the municipal parks.

It had been a year and a half since I'd moved to Lonesome Valley to start a new life after my husband Ned divorced me, married his assistant Candy, and became a father for the third time. Although it had taken me some time to gather my wits, make a plan, and strike out on my own to begin a new career as a full-time artist, I was happy I'd made the decision to move to Lonesome Valley, which was known all over the country as a vibrant art town. My daughter Emma and my son Dustin still hadn't quite recovered from the shock of their father's abrupt decision and its aftermath, but they were beginning to accept our family's new normal.

Oohs and aahs broke out from the group as the fireworks exploded in rapid succession, culminating with a truly spectacular display.

After the final colorful burst, we all clapped.

"Lonesome Valley did itself proud," Brian said. "Now that we've seen the show, I think I'll go get another burger. Would you like another one?"

"No to the hamburger, but could you please grab me one of those brownies on your way back?"

"Sure thing."

I was watching him making his way over to the grill when I spotted my friend Susan coming toward me.

"I got here just in time to see the fireworks," she said as she greeted me with a hug. "This year's show was the best ever!"

"Yes, it was wonderful," I agreed. "I was beginning to think you weren't coming."

"I was working on my tiger, and I lost track of the time."

"I can't wait to see it," I said.

Besides painting wonderful watercolors, Susan created huge, striking paper mâché animals. I smiled as I remembered Lola, a giraffe Susan had made. I'd seen Lola the first time I'd attended the Roadrunner's monthly session to change the artwork in the gallery. I'd just been accepted as a member of the cooperative art gallery the week before. Susan had been assigned to be my mentor, and we'd been friends ever since.

"I'm thinking of displaying my tiger at my Art in the Park booth next week, but I don't want to crowd things too much. Chip's going to share the booth, so I can't take all the space for myself. Plus he volunteered to do a painting demo, so we'll need some space for that."

"I bet you can make it work. Your tiger's sure to draw a lot of attention. Who knows? You might sell it right away. Your big paper mâché animals always go fast at the gallery."

"Hmm. You may have a point. I'll fit Tye—that's what I named him—in somehow. I'm sure Chip won't mind."

Susan's nephew Chip, a talented artist in his mid-twenties and a member of the Roadrunner himself, couldn't seem to decide which direction his art career should take. He'd dabbled in many media and styles but hadn't quite hit on his own unique vision yet. He always had a bit of a problem following through on his projects, and sometimes his unfinished paintings sat for weeks before he got around to completing them. In the meantime, he made a living working in his father's pizza parlor, and, with no rent payment at home, he didn't seem to be in any particular rush to move out of his parents' house into a place of his own.

"You actually missed some of the fireworks."

"How so? Did Rich break out his fountains like he did last year?"

"If only he had. I'm afraid he decided to shoot off rockets, and they went right over there." I pointed toward the house next door. "His neighbor didn't appreciate it. He and Rich would have come to blows if it weren't for Dave and Pamela's brother pulling them apart. Dave threatened them with jail if they didn't both settle down."

"I bet Rich didn't take that warning too well."

"He didn't. Look at him."

At the makeshift bar, Rich never looked up as he served drinks to Dawn and her mother Dorothy. When they drifted off, he slammed a glass down so hard that it shattered. We watched as Pamela picked up the pieces.

"That man has a temper," Susan observed.

"I'll say."

"What happened to the neighbor?"

I nodded toward the pool where Hal was lounging and sipping a margarita. "Pamela invited him to join the party. She made sure he filled his plate and had a margarita before he sat down, and he hasn't budged since."

Nor did he leave the spot he'd staked out next to the pool for the rest of the evening. Just before midnight, the guests began to depart, thanking Pamela and Rich for the party on their way out. As for Hal, he followed the crowd and left by the front door, just like everyone else, his exit much less spectacular than his entrance had been.

Chapter 2

Laddie, my golden retriever, was waiting to greet me as soon as I returned from the party. After I stooped to pet him, he stuck by me like he was glued to my legs. I inched my way toward the nearby sofa and plopped down. As I stroked his silky fur, he put his head on my lap.

"Rough evening?" I asked Emma, who always stayed with me during her summer break from college. In fact, I was sitting on her bed at the moment. My little house had only one bedroom, and Emma always insisted on sleeping on the hide-a-bed sofa in my dinky living room.

"It was. Laddie hated all the noise from the fireworks. He barked every time he heard a firecracker explode."

"Poor boy." I gave him a hug, and he put his paw on my knee before putting his head back down on my lap. "I suppose Mona Lisa hasn't come out yet?"

"Not a chance. She's still hiding under your bed. She's been under there ever since she heard the first firecracker hours ago."

"I bet she'll join you as soon as Laddie and I go to bed, speaking of which, I'm headed that way right now," I put my hand over my mouth to stifle a yawn. "I'm getting really tired."

It wasn't often that I stayed up past midnight, especially since I took Laddie for a morning walk at dawn every day, but late night or not, I doubted that he'd sleep in, although I was hoping he'd do just that, so I didn't set my alarm clock when I went to bed. Laddie settled himself on the bed with his chin on my feet. As soon as I turned out the bedside lamp, I heard Mona Lisa creep out from beneath the bed, and I knew she'd make a beeline straight to Emma. My calico kitty tolerated me and barely abided Laddie, but she favored Emma, and I was glad my daughter was home to comfort Mona Lisa.

It seemed as though I'd no more fallen asleep than I felt Laddie's paw on my arm, urging me to wake up. I groaned and half-opened one eye to look at the clock. Sure enough, it was five already.

With a second groan, I rolled out of bed, dressed, and we were off to the neighborhood park a few blocks away. Laddie pranced along happily, the lack of sleep not bothering him in the slightest. Of course, he could doze most of the day while I had work to do and couldn't afford the luxury of a nap.

I admit I was feeling a bit grumpy, but by the time we returned home, my mood had improved, and I was sure a few cups of coffee would help to motivate me.

Oblivious to us, Emma was still snoozing with Mona Lisa curled up beside her. I moved about my tiny kitchen as quietly as I could so I wouldn't wake her yet. She worked at the local feed store during her breaks from college and had to be there at eight. As soon as the coffee brewed, I poured a cup, and Laddie followed me into my studio, which was the same size as the entire rest of my house. Gently, I pulled the door closed, and Laddie lay down on his bed while I sipped my coffee and checked the email on my laptop.

An hour later, I was hard at work on a new landscape, done in my signature expressionistic abstract style, when Emma, still in her pajamas and holding a mug of coffee, opened the door to the studio.

"I'm going to jump in the shower now."

"Sleep well?"

"Yes, once Mona Lisa settled. The poor baby must have been terrified with all the noise last night. She's still asleep."

"Do you need the car, or are you riding to work with Dennis?"

"Going with Dennis."

Dennis and his wife Belle, who was my best friend, lived next door, and it was thanks to him that Emma had a job waiting whenever she was on a break from college. Dennis managed the feed store, so it was handy for Emma to ride with him to work, but on the days when their schedules were different, I either loaned Emma my SUV or dropped her off and picked her up from work, depending on my own schedule. Since my only firm commitment was to work two days a month at the Roadrunner, sharing my car with Emma wasn't a problem.

I'd spent years working with my ex in the office of his insurance agency, and now it felt like pure luxury not to have a fixed schedule. Of course, the downside was that I sometimes had to force myself into the studio to get some painting done, especially on days when I wasn't feeling particularly energetic. Luckily, this day was a productive one, and, fueled by several cups of coffee, I spent the morning and early afternoon painting, interrupted only by a couple of short breaks to let Laddie outside and to grab a sandwich.

After I finally stepped away from my landscape and put my oil paints away, I took the raspberry-chocolate pie I'd made for Belle and Dennis the day before out of the refrigerator where it had been chilling. After adding some fresh raspberries to the top, I drizzled on chocolate sauce, swirling it as I poured. I knew there would be no leftovers since Dennis had never met a pie he didn't love.

Tomorrow, Belle and Dennis were leaving on a trip to Michigan to visit their family, and they'd be gone for three weeks. I'd volunteered to keep an eye on their house and collect their mail, but since they'd be taking their little white dog Mr. Big along, Laddie would be deprived of his playmate until they returned.

I put the pie in a sturdy box and snapped Laddie's leash onto his collar. Leaving Mona Lisa to her own devices, we went next door, where Belle was waiting for us. She took the box from me, and we had no more stepped inside than Mr. Big began running around Laddie, and Laddie, eager to join in the fun with his pal, tugged on his leash. As soon as I released him, the two dogs raced to the back patio door, scampering outside after Belle set the pie down on the kitchen counter and slid the door open.

"Shall we have our pie on the patio?" Belle beamed, as she lifted it from the box. "Ooh, this looks delicious!"

"How's the packing coming along?" I asked after we went out to the patio with our pie and iced tea.

"Almost done. I'll pick up Mr. Big's toys to take along right before we leave in the morning. He knew something was up the instant we brought out the suitcases, and he's been guarding his toys. He must remember last time when I packed them early."

"He's sharp as a tack," I observed as we watched the dogs romp in the backyard. "Laddie's really going to miss him, and I'm going to miss *you*."

Belle smiled wistfully. "The time will go by in a flash," she said.

"You're not thinking of moving back to Michigan, are you? I know it's hard not being there with your family."

"It is. Our grandbabies are growing like weeds, but no, we're staying right here in Lonesome Valley. One thing about not seeing them so often is that's it's very special when we *do* see each other."

"And you don't spoil them at all, do you?"

"Who, me?" she chuckled.

It wasn't long before Laddie and Mr. Big, panting up a storm, joined us in the shade of the patio. The blazing Arizona sun beat down in the summer afternoons, and Belle's backyard enjoyed only partial shade at that time of day.

"By the way, I meant to ask you how the Fourth-of-July party was."

"It was fun, but there was a bit more excitement than we'd anticipated. Our host almost came to blows with his neighbor because Rich was shooting rockets over the guy's house. Other than that, it was great."

"Brian's back at work, I suppose."

"Yes. He actually drove back right after the party. He said there'd be way less traffic on the interstate than if he waited until this morning to leave. He'll be back home next weekend, and he's going to help me set up my booth at Art in the Park."

"I wish I could see it."

"There'll be plenty of other times. I just got accepted to exhibit in the Festival of the West in October."

"Amanda, that's great!"

"Yes, I'm happy I was accepted. It's one of the biggest juried art shows in the West."

We chatted for another hour or so before Laddie and I went home. I already had the key to Dennis and Belle's house so that I could check it and bring in the mail every day while they were on vacation. With Dennis away, his assistant manager Matt would be in charge of the store, and Emma would work more hours to help take up the slack. Considering that Matt was Emma's boyfriend, Emma didn't mind the extra hours one bit.

With Belle and Dennis in Michigan, Emma at work, and Brian out of town, I'd have more time to paint, but I'd have to push myself to do it because I had a terrible habit of procrastinating, given the slightest excuse, but I really couldn't afford to do that—not if I planned to have a full booth at Art in the Park.

Chapter 3

On a sunny Saturday morning a week and a half later, Emma, Brian, and I loaded his truck with the paintings I'd chosen to take to Art in the Park. Emma had the morning off, and since Brian was planning on setting up the tent and grids where I'd hang my paintings, she and Laddie were off to the park as soon as we'd stowed all the artwork in the bed of the truck.

Ralph, the oldest member of the Roadrunner, had offered to lend me his equipment since he hadn't signed up for an individual booth, preferring to help out at the Roadrunner's cooperative booth for a few hours instead.

The city park where the event was being held was bustling with activity when we arrived, and it soon became obvious that we'd have a trek from our parking space to my booth.

Ralph was supposed to meet us at the far end of the parking lot, and I spotted his big black truck right away, but, to my dismay, his tent and grids weren't in it, and there was no sign of Ralph, either.

"Oh, no," I groaned, pointing at the truck. "Ralph must have forgotten."

"Don't panic," Brian said. "Let's go ahead and unload the paintings. Then we'll look for him. I can always borrow his key and go over to his house to pick up everything."

"OK. I can't believe he forgot. I talked to him just last night."

"It'll work out," Brian assured me as we carefully placed several large paintings on the dolly Brian had brought. He moved the smaller paintings to the cab of the truck and locked the door.

As we made our way through the busy lot, I spotted Chip opening Susan's trunk.

"Chip, have you seen Ralph? He was going to lend me his grids, but his truck's empty."

"He's at the Roadrunner's booth, and he brought everything you need. In fact, we already set them up in your space."

"Oh, thank you! I'm so relieved."

Brian grinned. "Crisis averted."

"I'll say. My stomach twisted in knots when I saw his truck parked there with nothing in it."

"Your booth is right across from ours in Aisle Four, and the Roadrunner's booth is down at the end of the aisle. Besides us, Dawn and Dorothy are the only Roadrunner members with their own booth, and they have a double."

Dawn and her mother Dorothy owned a ceramics studio, so their artwork would be displayed on tables arranged in a "U" shape in their booth. I'd seen their set-up at other shows, and I'd marveled at how efficiently they set up their booth for art shows to show off their unique pieces featuring special glazes they produced themselves.

I felt like a latecomer when we reached Aisle Four and saw that most of the other artists' booths were all set up and ready to go, even though the event didn't officially start for an hour yet. I noticed a few browsers already milling around. At least we had a head start, thanks to Ralph and Chip, and I began placing paintings on the grids while Brian returned to the truck to pick up the rest of them.

Following a mock-up I'd drawn ahead of time, I finished hanging my artwork, but what had looked good on paper didn't always look the way I'd imagined when my paintings were hung on the grids, so I fiddled around, rearranging a few of the canvasses until I was satisfied. I'd also brought a small box containing several packets of note cards printed with images of some of my abstract landscapes and some silk scarves, each dyed with a unique abstract design. I'd learned that, much as a potential customer might admire my oil paintings, their prices could be a significant barrier to a purchase, so I made it a point to have some more affordable art available, too. While I set up the note cards and scarf display on top of the small table folding table we'd brought, Brian stowed the box under the table where it would be hidden by my cloth drape.

"Looking good."

I turned to see Ralph, who was standing in the center aisle behind me.

"I couldn't have done it without you. Thanks so much for lending me the tent and grids."

"You're welcome, Amanda. Anytime. A few hours at the Roadrunner's booth will be plenty enough of the show for me. I don't have the energy I used to."

After eliciting my promise that I'd drop by the Roadrunner's booth later for a quick peek at our co-op's display, Ralph limped back to the Roadrunner's booth, although he wasn't aided by the cane he sometimes used. I watched him go, and by the time he'd reached the Roadrunner's tent, a small group of people had gathered in mine, and the show was on as far as I was concerned, even though it still hadn't officially begun.

Brian stayed, spelling me when I went to the restroom and bringing me a couple of tacos around noon.

"You're sure you have enough to eat, Amanda? I can go back to the food vendors and get you something else."

"Thanks, but it's plenty."

I quickly ate the tacos and wiped my hands during a brief lull. I didn't like to be distracted by a big meal while potential customers were in the booth. It didn't look good for an exhibitor who was there to sell artwork to be eating, instead of talking to browsers, so I'd made it a point to grab a quick bite when nobody was there whenever I'd worked at the Roadrunner's booth.

"Are you sure you don't mind if I leave now?" Brian asked. I'd told him that he didn't need to stay all day.

"Of course not. I'll be just fine. If I have to leave the booth for a few minutes, Susan or Chip will keep an eye on it."

"OK, then. I'll check on Laddie and get a few chores done before I come back at five to pick you up." He gave me a quick kiss. "Call me if you need me before then."

"I will."

The crowd thinned a bit after Brian left, but the respite was followed by a steady stream of lookers who engaged me in conversation but departed without buying anything. I'd sold only one silk scarf since the show opened, and I was beginning to fear that it might be my only sale at the two-day event.

If so, at least I wouldn't be scrambling to pay my bills, as had happened during my first year as a full-time artist. My finances were on more of an even keel now, as least as much as they could be in a business with a lot of ups and downs.

Making sure I didn't rely on one venue or one type of artwork for my living had finally started to pay off. With representation at the Ian Adams Gallery in Scottsdale as well as the Roadrunner in Lonesome Valley, wholesaling my colorful, abstract silk scarves, opening my studio for Friday-night tours, promoting commissioned pet portraits, and participating in an occasional show, my eggs weren't all in one basket.

Still, I always felt more energized at a show when I had a few sales. I reminded myself that the sale of the one silk scarf had covered the very reasonable fee I'd paid for the booth rental, and I hadn't incurred any other expenses in connection with the show, so even if I sold nothing else all weekend, I wouldn't have lost any money. Art in the Park was well organized, the people I'd spoken to had all been pleasant, and the day was glorious—I'd just have to console myself with those thoughts.

As a new group of people entered my booth, I smiled and greeted them. At the same time, a small crowd had gathered at Susan and Chip's booth across from me. I remembered that Chip had scheduled a painting demonstration. I would have liked to watch, but I couldn't neglect my own booth.

When a tall red-haired woman dressed in a blue skort and t-shirt studied my portrait of a basset hound, I approached her and soon learned that she'd love to have a painting of her beagle. When I quoted her a price, I could tell that she was a bit taken aback, and she seemed to be thinking about whether or not she wanted to proceed with the commission.

"Would you consider a lower price?"

"No. I'm sorry, but the price is firm."

There might have been a time in the past when I would have negotiated the price, but those days were over. Considering the time I spent making sure each pet portrait I painted captured the personality of my subject and working hard to get every detail just right, I knew my price was more than fair. Still, I realized that someone who'd never purchased artwork might think the cost was excessive. In fact, I'd been known to say that I couldn't afford my own paintings, although I'd been referring to larger, more expensive works I'd done.

"Hmm. Well, I'll have to think about it," she told me. "If I decide to go ahead, how long would it take for you to complete the picture?"

"I'd allow at least three or four weeks, although I might be finished sooner."

She nodded, thanked me, and walked away, leaving me to wonder how I could have handled the situation better. Direct sales certainly had never been my forté, although I was a little better at it than I had been when I first joined the Roadrunner shortly after moving to Lonesome Valley.

As the afternoon wore on and I interacted with many more people, I temporarily forgot about my prospective customer, but I remembered her soon enough when she approached my booth half an hour before closing time.

"I decided I'd like to get a portrait of Betsy," she informed me.

"Oh, great! Do you live here in town? If so, I'd like to meet her."

"I thought you worked from photos," she said hesitantly.

"I can certainly do that, but I find that if I'm able to meet my subjects in person, it really helps me capture their personalities."

"I see."

"Whichever you prefer; it's totally up to you."

"OK, I guess I could bring her to your house."

"Better make it your house. I have a golden retriever, and he's very friendly, so he'd monopolize Betsy, I'm sure."

After she agreed, I went over my contract for commissioned pet portraits with her, and she signed on the dotted line. We set up a meeting at her house on the following week so that I could meet Betsy the Beagle, and Betsy's proud pet mom charged her deposit to her credit card. Like most of the other vendors, I had an app on my phone to instantly process charges, and a receipt would automatically be sent to her email address.

Her earlier hesitancy had evaporated, and she smiled as she waved good-bye and wandered down the aisle toward the Roadrunner's booth.

She wasn't the only one who was smiling. I was still grinning from ear-to-ear when Brian came to pick me up.

"Good day?" he asked.

"Only two sales, but I can't complain."

"You never know. Tomorrow could be even better."

"Let's hope so, but even if I don't move any artwork at all tomorrow, I'll still be very happy with this show."

Chapter 4

"Surprise!"

I turned and saw my daughter Emma approaching my Art in the Park booth at the end of the following day. It had been a busy Sunday, and I was pleased that my sales had exceeded Saturday's.

Emma's surprise, my golden retriever Laddie, pranced along happily by her side. As soon as Laddie spotted me, his tail began whipping around in circles like a helicopter rotor. I stepped out of the tent to give him a hug and began stroking his silky fur, which glistened in the Arizona sunlight like spun gold tinted with copper.

"Well, this *is* a surprise," I told Emma. "I knew staying here all day in the booth with me would be too much for Laddie, but I'm glad you brought him now."

"Mom, why don't you sit down for a few minutes? You look a little tired. There's not much of a crowd now."

"I think I will."

I took Laddie's leash from Emma and led him behind the table that held my art note cards and abstract dyed silk scarves.

Snuggling as close as he could get, Laddie sat at my knee and pointed his nose upwards, a sure invitation for me to stroke his throat. I ran my fingers through his fur from his chin, down his chest, to his tummy. He lowered his head as I petted him, then raised it again for a repeat performance.

"Only five minutes till closing time," Emma commented, as she checked her cellphone. "Brian should be here with his truck soon. I'll help him break down the booth while you watch Laddie."

"OK. I don't mind if I do," I agreed.

After two days of standing up while I greeted potential customers and chatted with them about my artwork, I was ready to take a break. Brian had suggested taking me out for dinner at Luigi's, our favorite Italian restaurant, after we dropped off Ralph's grids and tent. Although the outdoor art show in one of Lonesome Valley's larger parks had been fun and I'd made some nice sales, I was looking forward to relaxing over a glass of wine and a lovely dinner.

"I'll take these bottles over to the recycle bin," Emma said, gathering several empty water bottles from behind the table.

Mid-July in Arizona was no picnic because of the heat, and even though Lonesome Valley was at a higher elevation than sweltering Phoenix and usually fifteen or twenty degrees cooler, the sunny days could be quite hot. People liked to say that it was a dry heat, and there was no doubt the lack of humidity helped somewhat.

I didn't regret moving to Lonesome Valley a year and a half earlier, though. The pretty little town was known for its numerous art galleries, artists' open studio nights, and art shows, especially the prestigious, juried Festival of the West, which took place annually in October.

I looked up and saw that Susan and Chip were starting to take her watercolors down from their display grids. They paused when Pamela, who'd been at the gallery's booth all day, came over. I couldn't hear their brief conversation, but Pamela seemed to be in a hurry as she left Susan's booth and came to mine.

"Hi, Amanda. Did you have a good show?"

"Yes, I'm very happy with it." I was about to tell her what I'd sold, but clearly her inquiry regarding my experience at the show wasn't her objective.

"Have you seen Rich? He's supposed to help me break down our booth." Pamela's irritation with her husband came through loud and clear.

I'd seen Rich hanging around the Roadrunner's booth in the morning and early afternoon, but not since then.

"It's been quite a while since I've seen him, Pamela, but Brian and I can help you if he doesn't show up soon."

"Susan and Chip volunteered, too, but you all have your own booths to dismantle. I can't imagine why he's not back yet. He left to get a sandwich nearly three hours ago, and I haven't seen him since."

I spotted Brian coming down the aisle and waved.

"What's up?" he asked as he joined us.

"Did you see Rich on your way in? Pamela's looking for him."

"No, I didn't see him, but I saw his Hummer in the parking lot, so he must be somewhere here in the park."

"I wish I knew where," Pamela muttered. "I guess I'll look around for a few minutes. If I don't find him by then, I may have to take you up on your offer."

Brian looked at me quizzically as Pamela stalked off.

"Not a happy camper," he said, watching Pamela leave.

"I guess I can't blame her. I can't imagine why Rich isn't back yet. He knew that Pamela would be alone for the last hour of the show, but he was supposed to be there to help her out. Good thing it hasn't been too busy for a while."

"We'd better get started," Brian suggested. "The sooner we have everything packed up in the truck, the sooner we can go to dinner."

"Sounds good to me."

Emma had already taken most of the paintings down from the grids, and since I thought things would move along faster without Laddie vying for my attention while I worked, I suggested that Emma take him home. I gave my golden boy a pat and promised I'd see him later.

"Emma, why don't I bring you home some lasagna from Luigi's?"

"OK, and don't worry: I won't forget to feed Laddie and Mona Lisa." My persnickety calico cat Mona Lisa would be waiting at home to pounce on Emma's toes and remind her that it was time to eat.

Brian and I worked quickly to dismantle my booth, and we soon had the tent, grids, table, and all my artwork stowed securely in the back of his truck. We planned to stop at Ralph's before we went to dinner so we could return the tent and grids I'd borrowed from him, but first we needed to find out whether Pamela had succeeded in locating Rich.

We headed back and saw that Susan and Chip were still packing up their artwork. Pamela was nowhere in sight.

"Looks like you two are all set," Susan said. "Why don't you head out? We'll hang around and help Pamela."

"Yeah, go ahead," Chip urged. "We have plenty of time. Dad gave me the evening off."

"I think we should stay," I said. I was tired from my long day, which had started at five when Laddie and I took our early morning walk.

Still, I'd feel guilty if I didn't help Pamela. If we all pitched in, it wouldn't take too long to break down the booth.

"So do I," Brian agreed. "In fact, we'll get started on the Roadrunner's booth while you two finish up here."

The words were no more out of Brian's mouth than a blood-curdling scream pierced the air.

Chapter 5

As we all rushed toward the direction of the shrill outcry, the screaming was replaced by a loud yell for help.

Pamela!

I recognized her voice right away. It was coming from behind the
park's small bandstand.

When we went around to the back, we were greeted by a horrific
sight.

With a knife protruding from his back between his shoulder blades,
Rich lay sprawled, face down, on the hard ground. Pamela's screams
turned to sobs as she knelt over him, her hands covered in his blood.

Brian stooped to check Rich's pulse, but he couldn't find one.

We weren't the only people to run to the scene. A few seconds after
we arrived, some of the other vendors and late-staying customers ran
up behind us.

"Let me through," a short, stocky man dressed in jeans and a western shirt said firmly. "I'm a doctor."

The crowd parted, but after a quick examination, the doctor confirmed what we had feared: Rich was dead.

I took Pamela gently by the arm and tried to encourage her to get
up so I could lead her away from her husband's body, but she refused

to budge. When two patrol officers arrived a few minutes later, she was still kneeling in the same spot where we'd found her earlier.

The officers herded us around front and told us to sit in the bleachers and wait until a detective showed up. One of the officers stayed with us, probably to make sure nobody left the scene.

I knew Dave Martinez had been at the show earlier to bring his wife Dawn and her mother Dorothy some lunch, and I was hoping that he might still be on the grounds since he was much easier to talk to than the gruff detective Lieutenant Belmont, who was difficult to get along with, to put it mildly. Susan despised the man because he had once arrested her for a murder she didn't commit, and she'd spent one terrible night in the county jail.

No such luck, though. After what seemed a very long time, but was probably no more than a few minutes, Lieutenant Belmont showed up, surveyed everyone sitting in the bleachers, and scowled when he saw Susan and me, but he didn't pause before going around the back to look at the crime scene.

When he returned, he focused his gaze on Pamela's hands, still covered in blood. The lieutenant attempted to talk with her, but by this point she was almost hysterical, her body racked by sobs, and clearly in no condition to speak with anyone. Lieutenant Belmont frowned as Pamela rocked back and forth, wailing loudly.

He motioned to one of the patrol officers, and I could hear him say something about "hospital" and "blood," but the rest of their conversation was muffled. Susan and I were sitting on either side of Pamela, trying to calm her to no avail.

A few minutes later, an ambulance arrived. When the attendants approached her, she looked confused, but she allowed them to give her a cursory examination before they took her away, accompanied by the same officer Lieutenant Belmont had conferred with. I assumed that the doctors at the emergency room would have to sedate her.

"What's with you two, anyway?" Lieutenant Belmont growled, directing his comment at Susan and me. "Another murder and you're both here at the scene."

"We were here for Art in the Park," I said. "There's nothing unusual about exhibiting our paintings at a show. I hope you're not trying to imply that we had anything to do with Rich's death because you know that's utter nonsense."

"So you admit you knew the victim."

"Of course, all the artists at the Roadrunner knew him. He's our gallery director's husband."

"The woman with the bloody hands?"

"Yes."

"Figures."

"What do you mean by that?" I didn't pause long enough to let Lieutenant Belmont respond. "Rich was supposed to help Pamela break down the Roadrunner's booth and take the artwork back to the gallery. He wasn't around when it was time to pack up, so she went to look for him. We heard her screaming and came to find out what was happening."

"We all got here at the same time," Brian volunteered.

"Who's 'we'?"

"Susan, Chip, Amanda, and me."

"OK. I know these three. Who are you? Another artist?"

"No, I'm Amanda's boyfriend, Brian Hudson."

If we hadn't been at the scene of a murder, I would have been tempted to laugh at the look on Lieutenant Belmont's face when Brian revealed our relationship. Maybe I should have felt offended. Although the lieutenant was fifty-five himself, perhaps he thought I was too old to have a boyfriend. After all, I'd reached the mid-century mark at my last birthday. Whatever the case, Brian seemed to have stopped the lieutenant in his tracks, at least temporarily.

When he recovered himself, Lieutenant Belmont drew us each aside individually and asked us to describe exactly what we'd seen when we'd found Rich lying on the ground. We had to tell him that Pamela had been kneeling over her husband's body, but perhaps her action came as no surprise since the blood on her hands had been impossible to miss. I felt very much afraid that Pamela might be the lieutenant's one-and-only suspect.

After he finally told us we could leave, I turned to Brian and whispered, "I think we should go to the hospital to check on Pamela."

"Agreed. That detective has her in his sights."

"Poor Pamela—to find her husband with a knife in his back. No wonder she's so distraught. The last thing she'll be thinking about is the lieutenant pegging her as a murder suspect. If we can get to her before he does, we can at least suggest that she retain a lawyer."

"The sooner, the better," Brian said. "Let's head to the hospital right after we get the gallery's booth cleared out. We can drop Ralph's equipment off later."

"Don't worry about the Roadrunner's booth," Susan told us. "Chip and I will take care of it. Maybe you're wrong in thinking Pamela's the prime suspect, but after my own experience with the lieutenant, I doubt it. I sure hope she doesn't end up in the county jail tonight."

"Or any night," I agreed.

Chapter 6

"There's Pamela's brother," I said when we entered the emergency room at Lonesome Valley's only hospital.

I was familiar with the place because not only had I visited a couple of patients there in the past, but I also sold my abstract art silk scarves wholesale to the hospital's gift shop. Before we reached Nate, a woman wearing a hospital badge and a white coat came through the doorway leading to the treatment area and began to talk to him. We waited until she left before approaching him.

"How's Pamela?" I asked, hoping Nate remembered us. Although Nate lived in Lonesome Valley and ran a thriving plumbing business, we had never met until we went to Pamela and Rich's party on the Fourth of July.

"Amanda, right?"

"Yes, and Brian," I prompted, guessing that he may have forgotten Brian's name. I was surprised he remembered mine. Although Pamela had introduced us, we'd chatted only briefly during the party.

"She's under sedation right now, and I haven't been able to talk to her at all. The hospital notified me that she'd been admitted. Just now, the doctor said her vital signs are stable, and she should be fine, but that's all she could tell me. I still don't know what happened."

"I'm afraid it's bad news, Nate. Rich is dead. Pamela found him, and she was extremely upset."

"Heart attack?"

"Much more shocking. Rich was murdered."

"Murdered!" He shook his head.

"Maybe we should sit down," I suggested.

"Yeah. OK," Nate said, slumping as he dropped into one of the hard plastic chairs in the ER's waiting room. "I can't believe it."

"Could I get you some water or maybe a coffee?" I offered.

Nate nodded. "Sure, black coffee, thanks."

Brian sat down next to Nate while I wandered down the nearest hallway in search of a vending machine. When I didn't find one, I went to the hospital's cafeteria and bought a cup of coffee for Nate there. Before returning to the ER, I texted Emma to let her know that I'd be late, but I didn't tell her the reason. There would be time enough to relate the shocking story after I went home.

When I returned to the emergency room, I handed Nate his coffee; he thanked me and took a quick gulp.

"I feel so useless," he said. "I guess there's not much I can do until Pamela's able to talk. She'll need help with the arrangements, and I can't even begin to imagine what she's going to do about Rich's business. Last I heard some company in California wanted to buy him out, and he was considering accepting their offer."

"Uh, Nate. I think there may be something more immediate that you can help with," I said.

"OK, shoot."

"Pamela may need a lawyer. She found Rich's body, and I think the police suspect her of killing him."

"My baby sister? A killer? That is the most ridiculous thing I've ever heard! She adored Rich, although I'll never understand why. There is no *way* she'd stab him. No way."

"Of course not, Nate," I said.

"We do think it would be a good idea to retain counsel now, rather than waiting," Brian suggested.

"Unbelievable! This just gets worse and worse."

"I know it's a terrible shock," I agreed. I couldn't get the image of Rich lying on the ground with a knife protruding from his back out of my mind.

"That's for sure, but I'm going to get on it right away. My attorney only handles business matters, but I'll check with him to get a recommendation for a lawyer who practices criminal law."

"Good idea," Brian commented, and I nodded.

"Listen, I appreciate you guys coming by, but there's no need for you to hang around here," Nate said as he pulled his cellphone from his jeans pocket. "I'm going to stay and call my lawyer. Maybe he can point me in the right direction, and I can find somebody to talk to the cops tonight."

"I hope so," I said. "I'll check on Pamela in the morning."

"Thanks." Nate turned his attention to his phone and began scrolling to find his lawyer's number, so we quietly left him there alone in the waiting room.

We went straight to Ralph's house when we left the hospital. When his jovial inquiry about how the show had gone met with glum looks from Brian and me, we knew that he hadn't yet heard the news about Rich's murder, so we filled him in. He'd known Pamela ever since she was his art student during a summer break from college, probably at least twenty-five years ago, and he was stunned that the police could suspect her of killing her husband. When he mentioned that he and Pamela were the only artists scheduled to work at the Roadrunner the next day, I volunteered to fill in for her.

We stayed longer at Ralph's than I'd anticipated, and although we hadn't eaten dinner, neither of us was particularly hungry, so we decided to skip going to Luigi's. Brian had to return to the new solar energy facility he managed, so he had a long drive to southern Arizona ahead of him in the morning. He'd been on the new job for a couple months now and regularly commuted home after work on Friday evening and returned early every Monday morning. During the work week, he stayed at a small hotel not far from the solar farm.

The schedule didn't seem to bother him because, in his previous job, he'd worked on an offshore oil rig, four weeks on and four weeks off. He'd had to fly to Texas to take a helicopter to the rig, so his current commute didn't faze him in the slightest.

Brian parked his truck at the end of his driveway, and since my house was next door to his, we didn't have to go far to unload my paintings. I unlocked the door to my studio, which took up half my house, leaving a small, but cozy, living area for me, Laddie, and my finicky cat Mona Lisa.

Emma must have heard us at the studio door because the lights went on before I opened the door, and Laddie rushed to greet me, tail wagging. I set the paintings I was carrying against the wall and petted my golden boy. He seemed to sense my mood and tried to snuggle even closer.

"What's wrong, Mom?" Evidently, Laddie wasn't the only one who could tell I was upset.

"Oh, Emma," I said sadly, as I gave her a hug. "Pamela's husband Rich was murdered. She found him lying on the ground with a knife in his back."

Emma looked taken aback. "I saw Rich walking around when Laddie and I left."

Brian and I exchanged a glance. "Where did you see him?"

"Over by the bandstand. He was talking to some guy."

"It sounds like you saw him shortly before he was murdered. Was he arguing with the other man?"

"I don't think so, but I really didn't pay too much attention. The guy was kind of tall—over six feet like Rich—and he was wearing a Stetson hat and jeans."

"He may be the killer," Brian said.

Emma gulped. "I suppose so."

"Do you think you'd recognize him if you saw him again?" I asked.

"Possibly, but I'm not a hundred percent sure."

"We need to report this to the police. At least they'll have another suspect besides Pamela. Let's give Dave a call. This day's bad enough without having to talk to Lieutenant Belmont again."

Chapter 7

After phoning Dave to tell him about Emma's sighting, my daughter and I nested on the sofa in my tiny living room with Mona Lisa, my mercurial kitty, curled up on Emma's lap and Laddie snoozing with his chin on my feet. Brian had gone home to try to get some sleep before his long drive back to work in the morning, and Emma and I sat up talking until the wee hours. I didn't think I'd be able to sleep, but, finally, I decided to try, so we made up the hide-a-bed for Emma, and I said good-night.

After we climbed into bed, it wasn't long before I heard the soft sounds of Laddie's breathing. Although Laddie usually lay across my feet, this night his head was on the pillow next to me that Mona Lisa claimed as her own when Emma was away at college. I tossed and turned, unable to get comfortable because I found it impossible to get the image of Rich with a knife in his back out of my mind. I kept thinking about Pamela and worrying about her predicament. Lieutenant Belmont was a stubborn man, and once he'd set his sights on her as his prime suspect, he wasn't too likely to change his mind.

After a couple of hours of fitful sleep, I was awakened by Laddie, who nudged me with his nose. First light woke him, and he was eager for his morning walk to the park. Knowing I'd never be able to get back to sleep anyway, I rolled out of bed, quickly dressed, and slipped out the back door with Laddie so we wouldn't waken Emma.

Due to the high elevation of Lonesome Valley, it was pleasantly cool, as was usual for this time of day in July, although the temperature would warm considerably by midday. Laddie stepped along happily, his tail constantly in motion. There were a few other dog walkers at the nearby park we usually frequented, and we casually greeted them as we circled the perimeter, but I didn't stop to chat.

I felt so preoccupied with Rich's untimely death and Pamela's dilemma that I could think of little else. It was far too early to check on Pamela, but I intended to call the hospital later. I was hoping she'd been discharged and had gone home, but I feared it was just as likely that she'd be at the police station or even incarcerated in the county jail.

When we got back home, I saw that the lights were on in the living room. Before I could unlock the front door, Emma opened it, and I smelled the welcome aroma of coffee wafting my way. The walk, three cups of coffee, and a shower all helped me feel more alert, which was a good thing since I'd promised Ralph I'd join him at the Roadrunner because Pamela wouldn't be there.

The gallery was open seven days a week, and all the members contributed their time, usually their required two days a month, to running the gallery. Most artists split their days into half days, which was what I normally did, too, because then I had time to do some painting. I had a terrible habit of procrastinating and sometimes had to force myself into my studio, so any habit that didn't tempt me to put off painting was helpful.

Before I left for the Roadrunner, I called the hospital. When I gave the operator Pamela's name and asked to be connected to her room, she told me that nobody by that name was a patient.

Right away, I called Pamela's cellphone, but she didn't answer, and I was prompted to leave a message on her voice mail.

Nobody answered my call to her house, either, so I looked up Nate's plumbing business number. He didn't answer.

I was worried for Pamela, but there wasn't anything I could do at the moment since I needed to meet Ralph at the gallery so we could open on time at nine.

When I arrived, I saw Ralph parking his truck on Main Street, in front of the gallery. I pulled up and parked behind him.

Although Lonesome Valley's downtown area enjoyed quite a bit of business due to the town's popularity with tourists, Mondays weren't especially busy, and I anticipated a slow day, which probably could be handled easily by one person, but the Roadrunner's policy dictated that two members must always be present when the gallery was open, and we didn't deviate from our rule.

"Any word about Pamela?" Ralph asked as he unlocked the front door of the gallery.

"I tried to call her this morning, but she isn't in the hospital, and she's not answering her cellphone or her landline. I even tried her brother's plumbing business number, but my call went straight to voice mail."

"Maybe she's not ready to talk to anyone yet," Ralph speculated. "On the other hand, I hope it's not bad news."

"Me, too. If she's at the police station, it certainly wouldn't be good news."

"I suppose the only way to help right now is to make sure the gallery's running smoothly," Ralph said. "Let's look at the week's schedule, and we can call some of the members to fill in for Pamela."

"Good idea."

We quickly readied the gallery for opening and then turned to the task of finding members who would be able to cover for Pamela. We'd just filled in all the slots when the jingling of the bell on the front door—a bell Rich had installed himself—caught our attention.

I whirled around and was shocked to see Pamela, still dressed in her blood-stained clothing, standing in the doorway. She hesitated before wandering over to the counter near the cash register where Ralph and I were standing.

She wobbled a bit as she approached us, and I ran to her and caught her around the waist so that she wouldn't fall. It took Ralph a bit longer to reach her. Although he couldn't move as fast as he used to due to his arthritis, it was only a few seconds before he took Pamela's arm, and we eased her into the chair we kept at the cash wrap area.

She looked at us and whispered, "Rich is dead."

"I know, Pamela," I said. "I'm so sorry."

Ralph nodded and squeezed her hand.

It was as though she had no recollection that I'd been at the park when she discovered Rich's body.

"Why don't I take you home now?" I offered, wondering where her brother could be.

"Oh, Nate's going to drive me home. Where is he?"

"I'm not sure, Pamela. Let me give him a call." I tried his plumbing business number again to no avail. If Pamela hadn't been so dazed, I would have asked her for Nate's cellphone number, although she probably wouldn't have remembered it offhand, anyway, and she didn't have her phone with her, either.

"No answer," I reported. "We can try to get in touch with him after I take you home."

"But that would leave Ralph here alone. We need two members in the gallery at all times."

Ralph and I exchanged glances. Both of us knew better than to argue with Pamela about her point even though it was ridiculous to maintain our protocol under the circumstances.

"I'll get someone to cover," I said, reaching for my cellphone as I spoke. Luckily, Susan answered my call and agreed to come to the gallery right away. Although I was curious about Pamela's movements, I didn't ask her where she had been this morning and why she was still dressed in yesterday's clothes.

Ralph went to get her a bottle of water while we waited for Susan. When he returned, Pamela accepted the bottle, uncapped it, sipped the water, and put the cap back on it. She looked around the gallery and began to weep. Her trickling tears soon turned into a flood, and our efforts to comfort her only seemed to upset her even more. I felt helpless as I patted her arm and handed her several tissues.

She didn't stop crying until I saw Susan's car pull up ahead of Ralph's.

"Pamela, Susan's here. Let's go now," I urged. I grabbed my bag and pulled my car keys out.

She allowed me to steer her outside and into the front passenger seat of my SUV. I started the car and was about to pull out into the sparse traffic on Main Street when a white van with a Nate's Plumbing sign painted in bold dark-red letters pulled up beside me. Our windows were down, and Nate nodded when I told him I was taking Pamela home.

"I'll meet you there," he said and proceeded down Main Street. As I followed him, I quickly glanced at Pamela from time to time. She didn't move or say a word during the short trip to her house.

When we arrived, Nate parked in the semi-circular driveway, and I pulled up in back of him, right in front of the impressive carved wooden double doorway.

Surrounded by desert landscaping, Pamela's large single-story house, designed in typical Southwestern style, featured tan stucco walls and a red-tile roof. Besides the house, there was a detached studio in back where Pamela painted and displayed her colorful acrylic paintings. Pamela and Rich didn't maintain the large property, which also boasted a huge swimming pool, on their own. Instead, they employed both a landscaper and a housekeeper.

Mrs. Bramble, the housekeeper, must have heard us coming because she opened the door before we had a chance to get out of the car. She and Nate rushed to help Pamela, and I trailed along behind them, into the tastefully furnished living room.

Mrs. Bramble wasted no time urging Pamela to shower and change her clothes. Pamela nodded meekly and went off in the direction of the master bedroom while Mrs. Bramble directed, rather than invited, us to sit down and insisted on serving us coffee. Rather than argue, we complied.

"She's rather formidable, isn't she?" I commented.

"She may be little, but she's mighty. You don't want to get on her bad side; that's for sure," Nate agreed. "I'm so relieved I found Pamela. The cops took her straight from the hospital to the police station this morning, but somehow she managed to slip out of there. I haven't had a chance to talk to her at all."

"She's not thinking straight, but I'm not surprised she headed for the gallery. It's only a few blocks from the station, and, of course, she's there at the gallery most weekdays, so it's just part of her routine."

"I'm really worried about her," Nate said. "She seems so out of it. I don't want the police trying to question her when she's in a such a state."

I couldn't have agreed with Nate more, but I knew Pamela's reprieve from police questioning couldn't possibly last long. I expected them to show up at her door any minute; in fact, I was surprised they hadn't been waiting at her house when we arrived. Just as that thought skittered through my mind, we heard vehicles in the driveway. I peeked out through the spaces between the slats on the shutters in the living room and saw Dave Martinez and a young uniformed officer getting out of a police cruiser. Another cruiser parked behind them, and pulling up the rear was none other than Lieutenant Belmont in his own car. I looked at Nate uneasily.

"Cops?" Nate asked.

"Yes. I'd better warn Pamela."

"Go ahead. I'll stall them for as long as I can."

As I hurried down the hallway, I heard the doorbell chime, followed by loud banging, and I knew Nate wouldn't be able to wait much longer before he let them in.

Chapter 8

The door to Pamela's bedroom was open. Running her fingers through her damp hair, Pamela was standing in front of her dresser. She wore a sleeveless black linen sheath dress that looked a couple of sizes too big for her. She was so tiny that the effect was magnified. I'd never seen Pamela dressed in any colors other than earth tones. The stark black dress made her pale skin look even paler.

I tapped lightly on the door frame, and Pamela turned to me. She didn't seem as spacey as she had earlier, so perhaps her shower had revived her a bit.

"Thanks for bringing me home, Amanda. I don't know what I was thinking, coming into the gallery today. I have so much to do—I must get down to the funeral home to make the arrangements."

As soon as she said it, tears began to trickle down her cheeks, and she grabbed a tissue from a box on top of her dresser and began to dab her eyes.

"Oh, Pamela, I'm so sorry, but the police are here. They want to talk to you."

"I guess I'd better get it over with." Pamela sighed. She picked up a black linen jacket that had been lying on the bed and put it on. It must have been a match for the dress she wore because it was also far too big for her. She reminded me of a small child playing dress-up in her mother's clothes. "Could you stay with me?"

"Of course. I will if they let me."

She glanced at me, and, for the first time, I saw fear in her eyes.

We walked down the long hallway to the foyer to find Dave, Lieutenant Belmont, and three uniformed officers waiting for Pamela. As soon as he saw me, Lieutenant Belmont growled, "What are you doing here?"

"I drove Pamela home."

"Time to leave," he said to me, nodding toward the front door. He stared at Nate and said, "You, too."

Nate looked down at the lieutenant and glared, but he didn't budge.

"No, please, don't go," Pamela pleaded, grabbing my arm. "I want you and Nate to stay."

The lieutenant didn't look too pleased, but Dave Martinez jumped in then and asked Pamela if they could search the property.

"Don't you need a search warrant to do that?" Nate asked.

"Not if the homeowner gives us permission."

"Don't do it, Pamela," Nate told his sister. "They can come back with a search warrant, *if* they can get one."

"It's all right, Nate," Pamela said. "I have nothing to hide. Go ahead."

"I promise we'll put everything back just as we found it," Dave assured her, as the uniformed officers began their search. He was in a very awkward position, not only because he'd been a guest at Pamela and Rich's Fourth of July party but also because he'd known Pamela for years since his wife Dawn was a member of the Roadrunner.

43

Ironically, Dave asked us to wait on the very same back patio where we'd watched fireworks at the Fourth of July party while the officers conducted their search. Pamela, Nate, Mrs. Bramble, and I all exited the house through the den's sliding glass door. Lieutenant Belmont hadn't said anything else, but I knew he hadn't given up on interviewing Pamela, and I suspected it wouldn't be long before he'd insist that she accompany him to the police station for a formal interview.

"Were you able to find a lawyer?" I whispered to Nate while Mrs. Bramble attempted to comfort Pamela. It certainly seemed as though Pamela would need an attorney; the sooner, the better.

"Yes, but he's in court all morning. He said he would contact me as soon as he's free. I haven't had a chance to tell Pamela yet. I'd better let her know."

Nate walked over to Pamela and Mrs. Bramble who were standing near the pool and drew Pamela aside. Mrs. Bramble left them and came over to sit, facing me. The patio cover, which extended several feet from the house, kept the bright sunlight off us. The stylish designer outdoor furniture was comfortable and luxurious, and any other bright sunny day it would have been a joy to relax there and laze in the shade.

"Poor Pamela," Mrs. Bramble lamented. "She doesn't deserve this type of treatment. She wouldn't hurt a fly. Too bad I can't say the same for her brother."

"What do you mean?" I asked, shocked at her innuendo.

"Nate's been in trouble with the law before. He has a bad temper, and when he's riled up, watch out!" She leaned forward and lowered her voice. "He's been in jail a couple of times."

"You think he could have killed Rich?"

She shrugged. "I don't know, but Pamela certainly didn't do it. She loved her husband. Sure, they argued sometimes. What couple doesn't? Come to think of it, they argued yesterday morning before they left for Art in the Park—something about Chip, as I recall—but it didn't mean anything. They always made up whenever they had a disagreement."

I was about to ask Mrs. Bramble why Nate had been in jail, but before I had a chance, Dave stepped out of the house onto the patio and told Pamela that Lieutenant Belmont wanted to interview her at the station. She started toward Dave, but Nate took her arm and held her back.

"She's not saying a word until she talks to her lawyer, and he's in court right now."

Lieutenant Belmont slid open the patio door and poked his head out. "What's the holdup?" he asked Dave.

"Pamela wants to wait to be interviewed until after she's spoken to her lawyer, but he's in court this morning." Dave said.

"Who's your lawyer, Mrs. Smith?" Lieutenant Belmont asked. I couldn't believe how low-key the lieutenant was. Normally, he would have been extremely irritated under the circumstances, and his obnoxious manner would have kicked in long ago.

Pamela looked to Nate for the answer.

"John Aguilar, lieutenant," Nate volunteered.

"Hmm. Well, have Mr. Aguilar call me to set up an appointment as soon as he's done in court. I'll be expecting his call."

"Thank you," Pamela murmured.

The lieutenant left, and Dave lingered long enough to tell us he was going to check on the search, and we should be able to come back inside soon. We waited nervously until we were finally given the all-clear.

Mrs. Bramble, who'd declared that "the cops better not have messed up my kitchen," hurried to check on it. Her face pale, she returned in a few seconds, wailing, "They took my knives—my gourmet chef's knives!"

Chapter 9

My heart sank. I doubted that the police would have confiscated the knives unless one was missing from the set. Could the knife the killer used to stab Rich have come from his own kitchen? If so, the police would have another piece of circumstantial evidence that pointed to Pamela.

I wondered when Mrs. Bramble had last used her precious knives. If one of them had been missing for a week, wouldn't she have noticed it before now?

I couldn't stop myself. I just had to ask the question: "Mrs. Bramble, when was the last time you used the knives?"

"The Fourth of July, when I was preparing food for the party. I've been on vacation ever since. This is my first day back at work."

Clearly Mrs. Bramble, Pamela, and Rich weren't the only ones who'd had access to the kitchen; in fact, plenty of other people had been in the house during Pamela and Rich's Fourth of July party. It wouldn't have been difficult for a guest to surreptitiously remove the knife during the party.

As soon as Mrs. Bramble mentioned the party, tears sprang to Pamela's eyes, and she began to cry. Nate guided her to the sofa and sat down beside her while I looked around for some tissues to give her.

"In the kitchen," Mrs. Bramble told me, and I followed her and took the box of tissues she handed me to Pamela.

After her sobs ceased, I suggested that perhaps she should try to eat something, but she shook her head.

"How about some coffee then?" Nate said.

"Well, all right," Pamela agreed.

Mrs. Bramble returned to the kitchen, and I followed.

"Can I help with anything?" I asked.

"Yes, let's fix some sandwiches, too, even though Pamela said she didn't want anything. She barely eats as it is."

Mrs. Bramble set bread, cheese, lettuce, and condiments out on the kitchen island, and I started to assemble some sandwiches while she made a fresh pot of coffee.

"I noticed that her dress seems way too big for her, but she looks the same size to me as she was when I first met her last year. She's been tiny ever since I've known her."

"The last time she wore that dress was at her father's funeral eight years ago. About a year later, she went on a diet and lost quite a bit of weight. I think she's way too thin, but that's the way Rich liked her, and she wanted to please him, sometimes too much. Honestly, that man would get jealous over absolutely nothing."

"Really?" I prompted, although I'd observed some of Rich's jealous behavior myself. I knew he'd suspected that Pamela had had an affair with Chip. I'd thought so, too, after I'd accidentally seen them kissing at Pamela's studio door shortly after I joined the Roadrunner, but Pamela had since insisted that, although they'd shared a few passionate kisses, their fling hadn't amounted to anything more. It had caused problems between Rich and Pamela, though. More than once, Rich had had words with Chip, who tried to avoid both him and Pamela. Chip had given up his studio upstairs at the Roadrunner and re-arranged his schedule there so it wouldn't coincide with Pamela's, all in an attempt to pacify Rich, who'd wanted Pamela to resign as director of the Roadrunner so she wouldn't be around Chip.

"Didn't you say they argued about Chip Sunday morning, before they left for Art in the Park?" I asked.

"Yes."

"But I thought you didn't come back to work until today."

"That's right. I was here for only a few minutes yesterday morning. I just dropped by to pick up a few things. I don't think Pamela and Rich even knew I was here."

I had to think about her statement for a while. Mrs. Bramble certainly didn't act as though I'd caught her in a lie, and her story could be plausible.

I knew for a fact that Pamela and Rich had definitely argued about Chip at other times, so one more argument might not be significant.

However, Lieutenant Belmont could interpret their disagreement on the same day as the murder as a possible motive for Pamela to kill her husband. Although I didn't know for sure that a knife was missing from the set the police had taken away, I doubted they would have removed the knives otherwise. Then there was the uncomfortable fact that we'd found Pamela kneeling over her husband's body and that she'd had blood on her hands. The circumstantial evidence was mounting up, and it wasn't looking good for Pamela.

Chapter 10

Nate assured me he'd stay with Pamela until they heard from her attorney, so I called Susan to let her know I was on my way back to the gallery.

"You don't need to come back today," Susan said. "It's totally dead here." Then she caught herself. "Oh, I shouldn't have put it *that* way. What I meant was that nobody has been in since I got here. How's Pamela doing?"

"About as well as she can, I suppose. At least, she doesn't seem as out of it as she did when she wandered into the gallery this morning. The police searched her house, and Lieutenant Belmont wants to talk to her this afternoon, but he agreed to wait until her attorney's available."

"That's something, coming from *him*," Susan said. She'd never be a fan of the lieutenant.

After I filled her in on everything I'd observed while I was at Pamela's house, I asked, "Are you sure you don't want to go home? I can come back to the gallery."

"No need, really, Amanda. I'll see you here tomorrow."

I'd almost forgotten that Susan and I had both signed up for Tuesday morning as part of our regular floor duty at the gallery. I thanked her for the reminder, dropped my cellphone into my bag, and fished around inside it for my car keys. They'd become caught on a ripped interior pocket seam, and I was struggling to disentangle them when a gruff voice interrupted me. Startled, I dropped my purse, and everything inside tumbled out, except the keys.

I looked up to see a tall man wearing a western hat standing in the driveway. He seemed vaguely familiar. Then it hit me.

I'd seen him before, at the Fourth of July party. He was the neighbor Rich had almost come to blows with that evening. I remembered that the man had settled down after Rich promised to stop shooting rockets and that he'd spent the rest of the evening drinking margaritas.

"Sorry, I didn't mean to startle you," the guy said. I'd heard his name at some point during the party, but I couldn't remember it. "Here, let me help you."

"Thanks. I guess I was startled. I didn't realize anyone was there." Both of us began picking up items that had spilled out of my bag and dropping them back inside.

"I think we met at Pamela and Rich's Fourth of July party," he said. "I'm Hal Quinlin."

"Amanda Trent." We hadn't exactly been introduced at the party, but after the incident, which all the party guests had observed, I certainly recognized him.

"I saw the commotion over here—the cops and all—and I wondered what was going on."

"You haven't heard?"

"No."

"Rich is dead. He was murdered yesterday."

I thought I detected the hint of a smirk as Hal bowed his head. Then he looked straight at me and remarked "that's a shame" before ambling off toward his house next door.

He hadn't even pretended to be shocked.

Chapter 11

Thinking about how weird the encounter had been, I yanked my keys free, causing the pocket seam to rip even more. Then I hoisted my bag onto my shoulder, started my SUV, and set my cellphone on the passenger seat. Hal turned around as I stopped at the end of Pamela's driveway, and I picked up the phone, pointed it at him and, before he had time to react, quickly took his picture.

Seeing him in his Stetson hat made me think there was a very good chance he was the man Emma had spotted talking to Rich shortly before he was killed. If so, she might be able to recognize him from the picture I'd just taken.

When I reached home, Laddie and Mona Lisa were both at the kitchen door to greet me. Laddie joyfully ran circles around me, finally stopping for me to pet him, while Mona Lisa pounced on my feet and meowed until I picked her up. After a few seconds of cuddle time, Mona Lisa leaped down and scurried to her kitty tree, where she liked to keep an eye on things from her top perch. Laddie was jumping up and down, so I took him outside for a romp. I'd forgotten that Emma was working this afternoon and evening. She wouldn't be home until after nine, but I was eager to find out whether she recognized Hal. As soon as Laddie tired of chasing his ball, we went back inside, and I texted the photo to Emma. She didn't respond right away, but I knew she'd check her phone when she took a break later.

In the meantime, I intended to work on a commissioned pet portrait of a pair of German shepherds that needed a few finishing touches. I enjoyed creating paintings that captured pets' unique personalities, although the realistic style I used for my pet portraits differed considerably from the looser expressionistic abstract landscapes I was fond of painting.

A couple hours passed, and Emma still hadn't called or texted me. I was tempted to call the store and ask to speak with her, but I knew they might be busy, and I didn't want to interrupt her work.

Finally, my cellphone buzzed with a new text message from Emma, who thought Hal might have been the man she'd seen talking with Rich, but she wasn't positive. I texted her that I'd let Dave know, and the police could take it from there.

I hesitated, though, before calling Dave. There was no way I wanted Hal to find out Emma had seen him with Rich at the park Sunday. If he was the killer, I didn't want him to know that Emma existed. Unfortunately, I'd really called attention to myself when I'd taken his picture. It probably wasn't the smartest thing I'd ever done, especially since I'd told him my name. My studio was open every Friday evening as part of Lonesome Valley's weekly open art studio tour, and he could easily find out where I lived.

Fretting over my ill-advised actions, I thought about asking Emma to stay with my ex-husband, his new wife Candy, and their baby son in Kansas City until her classes resumed in the fall, but she'd already spent a few days with them at the end of the spring semester, and she'd felt uncomfortable and out of place. I realized that if I suggested a visit there, Emma wouldn't want to go.

Reluctantly I called Dave and told him that I thought Hal might be the person Emma had seen talking to Rich shortly before he was killed but that Emma couldn't positively identify him.

Sounding a little grumpy, Dave said that the police were well aware of Pamela's neighbor.

"I appreciate the intel, Amanda, but let us do our work. The investigation is ongoing."

"But I'm worried about Emma."

"Hal Quinlin doesn't know who Emma is. How could he? We certainly wouldn't provide the name of someone who can't positively identify him as the man seen talking to Rich before he was murdered, either to him or his lawyer, if he has one."

"Maybe he could figure it out, though. I'm on his radar now that I took his picture. I shouldn't have done that." I was mentally kicking myself for taking such a stupid action. If I'd wanted to show Emma Hal's picture, I probably could have easily found one on social media.

"I'd have to agree with you there," Dave said.

"Why? Is he a suspect?"

"Come on, Amanda. You know I can't comment on that, but, if I were you, I wouldn't worry about it."

"So you do know something?"

"Sorry, Amanda, I have to go."

I thought Dave was trying to tell me that Hal wasn't a person of interest, although he hadn't come right out and said so. I had to admit my mind felt eased a bit. Even so, I checked all the doors and windows to make sure they were securely locked, and I felt somewhat relieved to learn that Emma's boyfriend was going to take her out for pizza after work. He was a big, strong young man with four years' experience in the military, so I felt confident Emma would be safe with him.

I prepared a light salad for dinner, fed Laddie and Mona Lisa, and waited for Brian's call, which usually came between seven or eight in the evening when he was at work.

Sure enough, he called promptly at seven. He'd had a tough day at work and sounded exhausted. I caught him up on all the developments of the day and shared my concern about Emma's safety.

"Dave promised the cops wouldn't divulge her name, so I don't think she's in any danger," Brian said. "*You*'re the one I'm worried about."

Chapter 12

"Please avoid this Hal character like the plague! I remember how he acted at the Fourth of July party. Whether he killed Rich or not, he has a hot temper. It's best to steer clear."

"Don't worry. I plan on doing exactly that."

After my conversation with Brian, I planted myself in my chair and mindlessly watched television while Laddie curled up at my feet and Mona Lisa settled herself on my lap. If Emma had asked me the plot of the movie I watched, I wouldn't have been able to tell her because my mind was whirling with thoughts about who'd killed Pamela's husband. The one thing I was sure of was that Pamela hadn't done it.

Just as I had waited up for my daughter during her high school years, this evening I waited for her to come home safely to our cozy little nest. At eleven, my patience was rewarded when Matt brought her home. After I greeted him and we chatted for a few minutes, I excused myself and went to bed with Laddie at my side.

Of course, Mona Lisa stayed in the living room with Emma and Matt. I could hear my daughter and her boyfriend laughing and talking, but although I was having a hard time going to sleep, they weren't the cause of my restlessness.

Around midnight, I heard the distinctive little creak that the front door always made when opened or closed, and I knew that Matt had left. It became quiet in the house then, but I continued to toss and turn into the wee hours and felt no more refreshed when Laddie woke me than I had the day before.

I decided it was going to take about a gallon of coffee to get me revved up and ready to meet Susan at the gallery. By the time I arrived, I'd had four cups and I was beginning to feel more alert.

Susan was unlocking the gallery door when I showed up, right on the dot of nine. She didn't look any more rested than I did, and I knew she was worried about Pamela, too. Because Susan had been arrested for a crime she hadn't committed last year, she knew that Lieutenant Belmont didn't always get it right. Since he was in charge of the investigation, it would be up to him to determine the person to arrest for Rich's murder.

We'd just entered the Roadrunner and turned on the lights when Chip appeared and followed us inside.

"No way could I stay away from two beautiful women," he teased as he gave his aunt a kiss on the cheek. His playful banter fell flat, though, and I could tell that, although he was trying to lighten the mood, he wasn't in the best frame of mind himself.

"Hi, Chip," I said. "I don't think you're scheduled to work today, are you?"

"No. I came to move my canvases and supplies back to the studio upstairs. I've imposed on you long enough, Aunt Susan. I'm taking up half of your studio space as it is."

"I don't mind, Chip. I have plenty of room."

"I appreciate that, but now that Rich isn't around to object to my presence, I may as well go back to working in my own space. I can concentrate better that way."

Chip's comment about being able to concentrate better in his own space certainly rang a bell with me. I had a tendency to become distracted too easily when I should be painting. However, I admitted I was a bit surprised that he hadn't waited a few weeks or at least until after Rich's memorial service.

"I'm going to run upstairs and get my studio in order before I start hauling everything back up there," Chip said, and he was off to the second floor, taking the steps two at a time.

"I wish he wasn't in such a hurry to use his studio," Susan said, "and I hope he doesn't take up with Pamela again."

"You know about that?" I asked, surprised because Susan had never mentioned his liaison with Pamela before, and I hadn't heard anyone else gossiping about it, either. I'd assumed I was the only one who knew.

"Chip told me when he asked if he could use my studio instead of his space here. He said Rich was jealous and didn't want him around."

"Yes, that's true. There were a couple of times when I thought they might come to blows right here in the gallery, although Chip tried to be cool about the situation."

"Rich was still jealous. It's too bad our booth at Art in the Park was so close to the Roadrunner's tent because Rich kept walking past and giving Chip the evil eye. When Chip was doing his acrylic painting demo Saturday, Rich stood at the back of the crowd, making sarcastic comments. I have to hand it to Chip, though: he kept right on painting and explaining his technique and ignored Rich completely. Finally, another guy standing next to Rich told him to shut up, so he left."

"I didn't realize that happened. I mean I saw the crowd, and I knew Chip was scheduled to do a painting demo, but I was pretty swamped with browsers in my booth at the time, so I didn't notice."

We heard Chip on the stairs again. This time he bounded down them, giving us a weak grin as he strode past us on his way to get his canvases and supplies out of his father's truck.

"I'll give you a hand," I offered.

He bowed and opened the gallery door with a flourish so that I could precede him out the door, but I stopped short when I almost bumped into Lieutenant Belmont on his way in. I wasn't so much startled by the lieutenant, though, as I was by what he was holding.

Chapter 13

Lieutenant Belmont was carrying a painting, but I couldn't readily tell what its subject was because it had been slashed diagonally from end to end, making a huge tear in the center so that the canvas sagged.

Susan backed up, whether from the nasty surprise of seeing the ripped canvas or from the equally unpleasant surprise of Lieutenant Belmont's appearance; I wasn't sure which.

I drew my breath in sharply at the sight of the defaced artwork. Chip seemed even more shocked than I was.

"Oh, no," he moaned, staring at the ruined painting. "Where did you find that?"

"You recognize it?" the lieutenant asked. "That's why I'm here. I figured somebody at the gallery might know who painted it."

"I painted it," Chip said, "at Art in the Park."

"When's the last time you saw it?"

"Saturday. Pamela really liked it, so I gave it to her."

"You mean to exhibit in the Roadrunner's booth?"

"No. It was a present for Pamela."

"So you didn't see it again after you'd given it to Mrs. Smith?"

"No. I guess Rich didn't like it too well."

"What makes you say that?"

"Well, look at it. You can see for yourself. Pamela certainly didn't take a knife to my painting."

"When did you last see Mr. Smith alive, Mr. Baxter?"

"I don't know exactly. Sometime early Sunday afternoon."

"Are you sure about that?"

"Yes, I'm sure."

"I'd like you to come back to the station with me. I have a few more questions for you."

"I've already told you everything I know. It's all in my statement."

"Don't do it, Chip," Susan piped up, earning her a baleful look from the lieutenant.

Ignoring Susan, the lieutenant pressed on. "Mrs. Smith is a friend of yours, isn't she?"

"We're all friends at the Roadrunner."

"I'm asking for your assistance, Mr. Baxter. Don't you want to find out who killed your friend's husband?"

"Sure," Chip answered.

Susan shook her head vigorously as Chip hesitated, appearing to consider whether or not he should talk to the lieutenant at the station.

"Let's go, then." Lieutenant Belmont started to push the gallery door open, motioning for Chip to precede him.

"I don't think so. I'm not going anywhere."

"Suit yourself. I'll keep your lack of cooperation in mind."

"I *have* cooperated!" Chip said in frustration, but the lieutenant was already out the door.

Chapter 14

"You did the right thing, Chip. Remember how he treated me," Susan said, as we huddled together at the cash wrap.

"I haven't forgotten. I'd sure like to know what's going on. Do you think I'm a suspect now?"

"Chip?" We turned to see Pamela, who must have passed Lieutenant Belmont on her way in. We were so distracted that we'd ignored the door chime.

"Pamela, what are you doing here? You don't need to worry about the gallery. We have it covered," I assured her.

"I know, and I'm grateful. I just stopped in for a minute to check on things. I'm not planning on staying."

"There's nothing to worry about here at the Roadrunner, Pamela," Chip assured her. "Everything's fine."

"It didn't sound so fine when I came in."

"For some reason, the lieutenant wanted to question me at the police station. I can't stand the guy, and I already gave my statement, so I refused to go with him."

"He is kind of scary, but when he interviewed me yesterday, at least he was polite. I was sure he was going to arrest me, but he said he'd be in touch if he had any other questions, and then he offered to have one of the officers drive me home. Of course, that wasn't necessary because Nate was waiting for me."

"That's odd for the lieutenant," I said. "I've never known him to act polite."

"Just the opposite," Susan agreed.

"I admit I was surprised," Pamela said. "I was pretty much petrified during the whole interview, just waiting for him to say I was under arrest. Unfortunately, he still could."

"I have a feeling I'm in his sights now," Chip said, "but I have no idea why."

"Maybe he thinks you saw Rich slash your painting and got angry," I speculated.

"But we don't know for sure that Rich was the one who slashed it," Pamela protested.

"Yeah, right," Chip muttered, but as soon as he saw Pamela tear up, he relented. "I'm sorry, Pamela. I shouldn't have said that. I don't know who did it. I better get my stuff unloaded."

Chip walked out to his truck and started pulling boxes out of the back while Pamela went down the hall to her office and unlocked the door. She didn't close it behind her. I wanted to talk to her, but I thought I'd give her a few moments alone to collect herself, so I took turns with Susan, watching the gallery and carrying Chip's boxes upstairs.

When we finished, he stayed upstairs in the studio, setting up his canvases and organizing his paints. The gallery was still quiet. Not one customer had come in since we'd opened at nine. I figured it might be a good time to approach Pamela.

She was sitting at her desk, arranging and re-arranging paperwork in neat stacks, and she didn't notice I was standing in the doorway, so I rapped gently on the door frame. She looked up and gave me a wan smile, and my heart went out to her. She looked so lost and alone.

"Forgive me for disturbing you, but I wonder if I could ask you a couple of questions."

"Sure. Have a seat. You're trying to figure out who killed Rich, aren't you?"

"Yes, I am," I admitted. "I know you didn't do it, and I certainly don't believe Chip did, either."

"Thanks for the vote of confidence, Amanda. Now if only the lieutenant thought the same."

"I bet he does. I think he would have arrested you if he thought you did it. There is some circumstantial evidence."

"You think he's going after Chip?"

"Possibly." I paused before changing the subject. "How did your neighbor Hal and Rich get along?"

"Not well. They couldn't stand each other. You saw that for yourself at our party. Still, I can't picture Hal as a killer."

"Hmm." I decided not to share Hal's sly smile when I told him about Rich's death or the fact that Emma might have seen Hal talking to Rich at Art in the Park. "By the way, did you and Rich have an argument before you went to the park Sunday?"

"How did you know about that?"

"Mrs. Bramble mentioned it. She said Chip's name was mentioned."

"That can't be right. She didn't come back from her vacation until yesterday."

"She told me she stopped by to pick up something, and that's when she heard you arguing."

"Well, she's right about that. We did argue, but it wasn't about Chip. Rich wanted to let Mrs. Bramble go. He said her health insurance cost a mint, and he wanted to improve his personal and business balance sheets because he needed to take out a loan for the business."

"I don't imagine she would have been too happy to hear that," I commented.

"Not at all. Her policy covers her and her family. The insurance company keeps raising the rates. Her husband's had back surgery twice and may need to have another operation, and her son's on some kind of super-expensive medication."

Chapter 15

I didn't really have time to consider that stunning revelation because I heard the door chime, followed by chatter, and I had to leave Pamela's office to help in the gallery. A group of several tourists had come in together, and they kept Susan and me busy answering questions. When they were followed by more browsers, we took turns ringing up sales, pleasantly surprised by the unexpected rush of business on a Tuesday morning. We were so swamped I didn't notice Pamela slip out, but her office door was locked when I went to tell her that Ralph and Chip were taking over for the afternoon at one o'clock.

As I drove to the grocery store on my way home, I couldn't help speculating on the possibility that Mrs. Bramble had accosted Rich in the park or had sneaked up behind him. Since he was stabbed in the back, it was possible that he hadn't been aware of a threat coming at him from behind.

I also wondered why Lieutenant Belmont had the idea that Chip had been involved. He'd been working in the booth he shared with Susan all day Sunday, except when he or Susan left to take a break or buy water from the concessions stand.

When I left the gallery, my thoughts turned to more mundane matters as I headed to the supermarket. Normally, I would have done my grocery shopping for the entire week, but I'd forgotten my list, so I decided to pick up only what I needed for the next couple of days. Shopping without my list invariably meant that I'd forget an item I needed and have to make another trip to the store anyway.

After I checked out, I grabbed my bags and pushed my cart back into line with the others outside the supermarket before walking to my car. I was fumbling with my key fob so that I could open the hatchback remotely when I was startled by a deep voice behind me.

"Hey, little lady, let me help you with those bags."

I whirled around and jumped when I saw Hal grinning at me.

"I didn't mean to scare you," he said, but I wondered if that were really true. I had a feeling that was *exactly* what he had intended.

Hal reached for the grocery bags, and I reluctantly handed them over. I didn't see much point in refusing to let him help. I glanced around, and we were the only people in the parking lot, which had been bustling when I'd arrived at the store earlier.

I didn't want to do anything to get him riled, so I thanked him as he closed the back.

"You bet, little lady. I figured you could use a hand, especially since you liked me well enough to take my picture yesterday. What was that all about?"

I looked down at the pavement. I definitely didn't want to tell him why I'd taken his photo. As I was wondering whether he suspected there was a method in my madness, he said, "Don't tell me you think I'm a suspect in Rich's murder."

My expression must have given me away. I was never very good at hiding my emotions.

"You *do*!"

I didn't confirm his statement, but he pressed on.

"Lady, I don't know you, and you don't know me, but I've got to tell you that just because I didn't get along with my neighbor doesn't mean I did away with the guy. I wasn't even in town Sunday. I was at a conference and awards ceremony in Vegas. Check it out if you don't believe me. Right about the time Rich was killed, I was at the Bellagio giving my acceptance speech for Innovator of the Year from the Southwest Growers Association."

He held my gaze for a moment before speaking again.

"Good day to you, ma'am."

With that, he tipped his hat and ambled off, toward the store, leaving me staring at him. I realized I'd missed an opportunity to find out more, but I'd been so nervous at having him show up and confront me that I'd literally been speechless.

It shouldn't be too difficult to confirm that he'd been out of town on Sunday afternoon, however. He'd invited me to "check it out," and that's exactly what I intended to do.

Chapter 16

As soon as I'd stashed my groceries, eaten lunch, and shared some playtime with Laddie and Mona Lisa, I sat down at my tiny dining table, opened my laptop, and began my research. It didn't take me long to find him online, see that he was involved in numerous business enterprises, and confirm that the Southwest Growers Association had held its annual convention in Las Vegas over the weekend and that Hal had indeed been named Innovator of the Year by the organization for the new irrigation system he'd designed.

It was more difficult to determine when he'd actually accepted the award, but I finally found a schedule that announced an awards ceremony at one o'clock. Since drive time from Las Vegas to Lonesome Valley was about four hours and we'd discovered Rich's body shortly after Art in the Park closed at five, it seemed highly unlikely, if not downright impossible, for Hal to have returned to Lonesome Valley in time to stab Rich.

Also, drive time wouldn't be the only factor. I doubted that Hal would have abruptly left the ceremony right after receiving his award. More than likely, he would have stuck around for a while to talk with members of the Growers' Association. Then there would have been the nightmare of making his way through Las Vegas traffic to get on the road on a Sunday when lots of tourists would be leaving town.

Just to confirm what I'd already learned, I checked Hal's social media profiles, and there was a picture of him accepting his award at the ceremony. So much for Hal as a suspect. At least I didn't have to worry about his finding out that Emma thought he might have been the man in the park she had spotted talking to Rich shortly before his death. It was a relief to know that my daughter was in no danger from Hal.

Rubbing my neck to get the kinks out, I stood and went to the refrigerator to get a drink. Laddie, snoozing beside me, didn't move until he heard me open the fridge door, and then he showed up right away. I poured myself a glass of limeade and dropped a couple of baby carrots into his bowl. He happily crunched and swallowed them. It took him only a few seconds, but he was satisfied.

Mona Lisa ignored the entire transaction, preferring to regard us disdainfully from her perch on top of her kitty tree.

Sipping the limeade, I returned to the table, set my glass down, and resumed my research, this time looking into others' social media profiles.

Chip's featured mainly images of his artworks and announcements about events at the Roadrunner. I smiled as I looked at some of the pictures he'd posted shortly after I'd first joined the Roadrunner. In a group photo of all the Roadrunner members, Chip stood in the middle row, in back of Susan and Pamela, with Dawn, Dave's wife, on one side of him and Dorothy, Dawn's mother, on the other side. We were all smiling broadly, and we looked as though we didn't have a care in the world. Chip's blond hair had been long then, and he'd tied it back in a ponytail. Now that he'd cut it, I thought he looked older, less like a teenager, although he still acted a bit like one at times.

I wouldn't have known Pamela was an artist from her sparse profile, but since the Roadrunner had its own website, her paintings were displayed there. She sold plenty of her artwork at the gallery and during Lonesome Valley's Friday night art studio tours. It looked as though she hadn't logged on to any personal social media sites in months. Even before that, she evidently hadn't been very active online.

Her brother Nate had no personal accounts that I could find, but he did have a profile and a website for his plumbing business.

Mrs. Bramble was active on several sites, and she'd posted numerous family photos with her husband, son, and daughter. She'd also shared hundreds of recipes with tips about how to make each of them successfully, leading me to believe she was quite a serious chef. Her husband's page was full of chat about his back problems, surgeries, and story swaps from his friends and relatives about their own health issues.

Except for my examination of Hal's social media profiles, my research hadn't revealed anything of interest. I closed my laptop. As soon as I rose, Laddie jumped up, ready to follow me. The day was warm, but not unbearably so, and I decided to take a short walk around the neighborhood.

I donned a floppy wide-brimmed hat, slathered on some sunscreen, put on my sunglasses, snapped Laddie's leash onto his collar, and we set off strolling, rather than walking at the rapid pace I preferred on our early morning jaunts.

As we walked, I thought about Rich's murder and tried to puzzle out the solution to who had killed Pamela's husband. After a few blocks, we turned around and headed back home. The day was hotter than I'd realized, and by the time we reached the air-conditioned comfort of my house, Laddie was panting and I was perspiring profusely.

As soon as I took his leash off, he bounded over to his water bowl and began drinking. When he was finished, he lay down on the tile floor in the kitchen to cool off while I fanned myself with my hat and poured another glass of limeade.

As I sipped it, suddenly the pieces of the puzzle seemed to fall into place. The more I thought about it, the surer I felt that I had the answer. There was only one problem: there wasn't a shred of evidence.

Chapter 17

The more I reflected on my theory, the more I felt certain I was on the right track, but the only way I could think of to bring the killer to justice was to encourage a confession since there wasn't really any solid evidence that I was aware of. I knew I should alert the police, but I doubted that Lieutenant Belmont would take kindly to my plan. Still, I had to try.

Leaving Laddie with a promise that "Mommy will be back soon," I drove to the police station and asked for Dave at the reception area. If he bought into my plan, maybe Lieutenant Belmont might go along with it, although I realized that obtaining the lieutenant's cooperation was a long shot at best.

I had only one thing going for me. I believed that Lieutenant Belmont had eliminated Pamela as a suspect. Otherwise, he surely would have arrested her by now. Of course, I could be totally wrong about that. I was basing my assumption on his actions in previous cases.

The lieutenant had always hated my "butting in," as he put it, but he'd reluctantly accepted my help a time or two. Despite his grouchy attitude, dour demeanor, and sarcastic comments to me, I was certain he wanted to arrest the right person for Rich's murder.

The officer on duty at the reception area had to answer a couple of phone calls before he was able to let me know that Dave wasn't in at the moment, and he didn't know whether he'd be back or not. That left me with only one option since I wouldn't be able to soften up the lieutenant by asking Dave to run interference.

I braced myself to speak to the lieutenant directly when the officer said I should go on down the hallway to his office.

The lieutenant groaned as soon as he saw me in the doorway.

"Well, if it isn't Nancy Drew. Go on. Sit down," he said, a look of resignation on his face. "What is it this time?"

"I think I know who killed Rich Smith," I said.

"Of course you do," he said with a sigh. "And I suppose you're going to tell me all about it."

Before he could object again, I proceeded to do just that. To my amazement, he looked thoughtful after I explained my reasoning and my plan.

"OK, I'm going to go along with your little charade because you may have a point and the chief's insisting on an arrest pronto, but. . . ."

"Yes?"

"If this turns out to be a giant waste of time, you're going to stand down and leave the investigating to me. Do I make myself clear?"

"Perfectly," I said, secretly pleased that he'd bought into my idea.

Chapter 18

Parting the curtain slightly, I glanced nervously out my front window. Now that my plan was in place, I wondered if I was really ready for showtime and whether my idea would work or fail. If it failed, not only would I never hear the end of it from Lieutenant Belmont, but I'd also pledged to leave the detective work to him.

The house was quiet except for the drip-drip-drip sound of water droplets plopping into the pail under my kitchen sink. I'd asked Emma to take Laddie to the park, and silence reigned without the two of them. Of course, Emma wasn't home much of the time, anyway, but I was used to having Laddie and Mona Lisa, my constant companions, by my side. Even though Laddie wasn't particularly noisy, except for occasional barking, his exuberant presence made our abode livelier. Mona Lisa had deserted me to hide under the bed as soon as our visitors arrived, so there wasn't even a plaintive meow to break the silence.

Lieutenant Belmont had stationed himself just inside the door to my studio, which we'd left slightly ajar. Two other officers were posted inside the garage. Because my house was so small, they would be able to hear any conversation, although I wasn't sure there would be one since I was becoming more and more doubtful about my ability to draw out the killer, who should be arriving any minute.

Just as I was about to drop the curtain back into place, a van pulled up at the curb. I took a deep breath and put on my game face as I swung open the front door.

"Hi, thanks for coming," I said. "I know it's a minor thing, but it's quite annoying."

"No problem. Let's have a look."

"Over there," I said, indicating my tiny kitchen, where I'd left the cabinet door under the sink open.

After ducking his head into the small space, Nate informed me that the leaky pipe was corroded and needed to be replaced. He quoted me a price, and I told him to go ahead with the work. While he went out to his van to get a replacement, I paced back and forth, worrying about whether I could get him to talk.

When he returned, I sat at my little dining table, only a few yards from where he was working. I tried to initiate a conversation a couple of times, but his one-word answers didn't encourage follow-up, and I decided to wait until he was done installing the pipe.

Finally, he announced that I was "all set." I wrote him a check, and he handed me a receipt. I felt a bit panicked. I hadn't taken advantage of my opportunity, which was going to slip away in a minute if I didn't do something right away.

"How's Pamela holding up?" I asked, even though I'd seen her only yesterday.

"Not too well," he responded. "She's afraid she might be arrested any time."

"It's a shame."

"Pamela told me you know Lieutenant Belmont. Do you really think he might arrest her?"

"I think it's a distinct possibility. He arrested my friend Susan and put her in jail last year on far less evidence. I hope the same thing doesn't happen to Pamela."

Nate seemed to be considering my words, but he didn't reply. If our ruse didn't inspire him to confess, probably nothing else I could say would. I had to force myself not to look at my phone, which I'd deliberately left on the table nearby so that I could grab it quickly as soon as Dave made his prearranged call to me.

As soon as it rang, I scooped it up.

"Hello," I answered, trying not to give away that I'd been expecting the call. I paused to let Dave speak.

"Could you repeat that, Dave?" I asked as I put the phone on speaker mode and held it up for Nate to hear.

"I said Pamela's about to be arrested! We're making arrangements with her lawyer now for her to surrender herself. She'll need all the support she can get. You may be able to visit her at the county jail tomorrow. I can get back to you on that."

"Yes, please let me know," I said weakly, tapping the phone to end the call." Turning to Nate, I asked, "You heard all that, right?"

Nate nodded. "I have to get over to Pamela's right now."

"I think you can do more than put in an appearance."

"What do you mean?"

"I think you know what I mean, Nate. Are you really going to let the police arrest an innocent woman?"

"I can't stop them."

"Yes, you can. Admit that you're the one who killed Rich."

"I didn't."

"Are you really willing to let Pamela go to prison for a crime *you* committed? I thought you loved your sister."

"I do love her." He took a step toward me, and I backed away.

"Then why don't you do the right thing and spare her more of an ordeal than she's already going through? You know as well as I do that Rich was the love of her life. It's bad enough that she lost her husband, but now she might spend the rest of her life in prison."

"I didn't mean to do it."

"Do what?"

"Stab Rich. I never planned to kill him. We ran into each other and got into a stupid argument. My temper got the better of me. I just sort of lost control for a few seconds. Rich and I may not have been best buddies, but I'd never intentionally do anything to hurt my baby sister."

It seemed like a million years before all three officers descended on Nate, who didn't put up any resistance, but it must have been mere seconds.

Before I knew it, the hapless plumber had been handcuffed, and Lieutenant Belmont was reciting the first part of the Miranda rights statement. After that, he continued with the two questions at the end.

"Do you understand the rights I have just read to you? With these rights in mind, do you wish to speak to me?"

Hanging his head, Nate nodded.

"I need to hear you say it."

"Yes, I understand, but I'm not saying another word," he mumbled. "I want to call my lawyer."

Chapter 19

We waited after Lieutenant Belmont directed one of the officers to bring a patrol car to pick up the suspect. True to his word, Nate didn't say a thing as he stood sandwiched between two burly uniformed officers. As soon as the cruiser arrived, they marched Nate outside. I followed them out, onto the front stoop, and watched as they maneuvered Nate into the back seat of the patrol car and closed the door.

My next-door neighbors weren't home, but a few others across the street came out to see what all the commotion was about. I was afraid some of them might come over to ask me what had happened, but I really didn't want to discuss it with them.

I'd begun to back up, toward my front door, when I saw Emma and Laddie coming around the corner. As soon as she saw the police activity, she broke into a jog. Jogging was a fun game for Laddie, and he kept pace right alongside her. In less than a minute they'd joined me by the front door.

"What's going on, Mom?" Emma asked, panting as Laddie pranced with excitement and jumped up on me to give me a hug. It was a habit I tried to discourage, but whenever he was super-excited, I gave in and hugged him back. He was so adorable that I found him impossible to resist.

"Nate's been arrested for killing Rich," I said.

"The *plumber*?" she asked incredulously. Nate's van was still parked out front, and Emma knew I'd been waiting for a plumber to arrive to fix the leak under the kitchen sink.

"Yes, the same, but he's not only the plumber; he's also Pamela's brother."

"What happened, Mom? How come he was arrested *here*?"

"It's a long story, Emma. Let's go inside before one of the neighbors comes over to give me the third degree."

Before we had a chance to go into the house, Lieutenant Belmont came up the steps to talk to me.

"Looks like we got our man," he said gruffly. "I have a feeling this won't go to trial. Most likely the district attorney will come up with a plea deal, but we'll see. In any case, I'll need you to make a statement. You know the drill. You can come in tomorrow and do it then."

"But you have a recording, right?"

"Yup, but we still need your statement. Have to cross the t's and dot the i's. You ought to know that by now."

"All right," I agreed reluctantly, not looking forward to getting further involved in the case. I had the sinking feeling that Pamela wouldn't be too happy with me for playing a part in her brother's arrest, even though Nate was responsible for Rich's death. I was actually quite sad that Nate had turned out to be the killer. I didn't think he was an evil man, but a guy who had blind rages and couldn't control his temper. It had gotten him into trouble before, but nothing like the trouble he was in now.

"By the way, if Nate hadn't confessed, I really *would* have had to arrest his sister. The chief's demanding action."

I can't say this bit of news made me feel much better, but it would have been truly awful if Pamela had been arrested.

After Lieutenant Belmont left, I stooped to unhook Laddie's leash from his collar and stroke his soft fur.

"Did you and the cops set Nate up?" Emma asked, after a few seconds.

"I suppose you could put it that way. I thought he'd killed Rich, but there was no proof. As far as I know, there's still no physical evidence to connect him to the murder. So a confession was the only way."

"Oh, Mom, that could have been dangerous," Emma said, flinging her arms around me in a tight hug.

"I'm sorry, honey, but I'm fine. I didn't think I'd be in any danger because the police were here all along, hidden in the studio and the garage. They could hear everything Nate and I said. I felt safe enough."

Emma shook her head, but she gave me a little smile.

"Am I forgiven?"

"I suppose so, but don't do something like that again, OK?"

"I think this was a one-off."

"It better be! How did you figure out Nate killed Rich?"

"It came down to three things, but, like I said before, there was absolutely no proof, just common-sense reasoning. First, he may have slipped up. When Brian and I saw Nate at the hospital right after the murder, I told him Rich was dead. I didn't tell him how he'd been killed, but a few minutes later Nate commented that Rich had been stabbed. It's possible that Brian told him after I went to get Nate a cup of coffee, so I couldn't be positive. Unfortunately, I didn't think to ask Brian the last time I talked to him. When I tried to call him to find out, he was tied up in meetings.

"Another thing was that Nate has a record. He's been arrested before, according to Pamela's housekeeper. The man has a temper, and when he becomes angry, he can be violent.

"And last, but not least, it just doesn't make sense that Pamela could have stabbed Rich. You know how tiny she is, and he was a tall man. To stab him between the shoulder blades, she would have had to reach up like this." I paused to demonstrate. "See how awkward that would be? There's no way she'd have the leverage to do it, so it had to be someone much taller."

"But I thought you suspected Pamela's neighbor Hal."

"I did for a while, but it turned out he had an alibi for the time of the murder. He wasn't even in town."

"So I guess he isn't the man I saw arguing with Rich, after all."

"Evidently not."

"My mother, the detective. Are you sure you wouldn't rather be an artist?"

"And how. Speaking of which, I'd better get back to the studio. That pet portrait I've been painting won't finish itself!"

Chapter 20

"Amanda, Nate is in jail!"

When my cellphone rang, I'd felt tempted to ignore Pamela's call, but, of course, that would have been the cowardly thing to do. I was very much afraid that my friend wouldn't appreciate the part I'd played in her brother's arrest.

"I know. I'm sorry, Pamela."

"How did you know? I've only just found out myself."

I hesitated. I really didn't want to have this conversation with Pamela, but if I didn't tell her, I knew that Nate would.

"He was arrested at my house."

"Your house?"

"Yes, he came to fix a leaky pipe under my kitchen sink."

"I still don't get it. Did his dispatcher tell the cops where he was working?"

I took a deep breath before replying: "He confessed to stabbing Rich, Pamela."

"That's impossible. Why would he do that?"

"He said he did it. I heard him."

"Wait a minute. What's going on here? You had something to do with it, didn't you?"

"Well, I. . . ."

I was about to explain that I'd told Lieutenant Belmont my suspicions about Nate, but she hung up on me before I had the chance.

I set my cellphone down on my desk in the studio, cleaned my brushes, and put my paints away. I hoped that Pamela would eventually understand that I'd been trying to help her, but I wasn't holding my breath.

I felt terrible that Pamela had lost both her husband and her brother and that I might have lost her as a friend, too.

When Laddie nudged me with his nose, I glanced at the clock and saw that it was past time for his dinner. The thought of food hadn't crossed my mind. Emma had left earlier for the second half of a split shift at work, Laddie and Mona Lisa had both been snoozing, and I'd been trying to concentrate on my painting, despite my mixed emotions about Nate's arrest. Pamela had reacted much as I'd feared, and I guessed I couldn't blame her.

I thought about the first time I'd met her at my interview when I'd applied to join the Roadrunner as a member artist. As a board member, she was part of the committee to make the decision on my membership. Although none of the board members had been especially encouraging during my interview, they'd accepted me the next day. To my surprise, Pamela had turned out to be very helpful to me when my studio had been left off the map for the Lonesome Valley Friday Night Art Studio Tour, and we'd been friends ever since.

Laddie whimpered softly, and I pulled myself out of my reverie enough to stroke his silky fur.

"OK, Laddie. I get the message."

Mona Lisa had crept into the kitchen, too, in anticipation of her evening meal. She looked up at me and meowed.

"You, too, Mona Lisa. Coming right up."

I cleaned their bowls, measured their food, and set their dishes down at opposite corners of the kitchen. They wasted no time in eating their kibble. Laddie was licking his bowl when Mona Lisa sashayed past him, taking a swipe at his tail as she went by. Startled, Laddie looked up for a second, but he didn't retaliate. It was a good thing he was such a laid-back boy. In the meantime, Mona Lisa leapt to the top of her kitty tree and turned her back on both of us.

"Et tu, Mona Lisa?" I murmured, although her behavior wasn't unusual.

I had to admit that I was really bothered by Pamela's abrupt hang-up. Still, even if I'd explained exactly how Nate came to confess to stabbing Rich, I doubted that she would have reacted much differently. Maybe in time she'd come to realize that I'd been trying to help her. At least, I hoped so.

I was still stewing over my conversation with Pamela when Brian called half an hour later.

"Nate? Really?" Brian said after I told him about Nate's arrest.

"I know. I didn't want to believe that he killed Rich, but he did confess."

"I'm blown away. He seemed so concerned about Pamela when we saw him at the hospital."

"He certainly did. That reminds me: I wanted to ask you something, and I tried to call you about it, but you were tied up in meetings. When I went to get Nate coffee at the hospital, did you tell him that Rich was stabbed?"

"I think you told him he was dead—that he'd been murdered—when we first got there."

"Right, I remember that, but I never mentioned how. Did you happen to tell him when I left the waiting room?"

"Let's see." Brian paused. "I may have. I can't really remember. Why?"

"It's just that he mentioned it himself before we left him there at the hospital. It would have been a red flag if he hadn't learned about it from somebody else. I should have noticed and checked with you at the time, but I was so upset, I didn't catch it then. It only occurred to me later. It's a good thing he confessed because there isn't really any physical evidence connecting him to the murder unless the police have found something since Nate's arrest."

"I guess he didn't know that. Otherwise, why would he confess?"

"He didn't want his sister to go to jail. We kind of let it be known that Pamela was about to be arrested."

"Was she?"

"Not right at that moment. That part wasn't true, but she probably would have been soon. The lieutenant admitted that he was getting pressure to make an arrest, and Pamela was the one who found Rich right after he'd been stabbed. We all saw her kneeling over his body."

"With bloody hands."

"It was awful. I'll never forget it. Poor Pamela! And to find out her own brother killed Rich. It's like a nightmare that goes on and on. I hope Nate's lawyer can negotiate a plea deal, so Pamela doesn't have to sit through a trial."

"Since Nate confessed, a plea deal seems likely."

"I just hope Pamela will forgive me."

"You were the messenger, not the killer. Surely she'll come to understand that."

"I hope so. In the meantime, I doubt that she'll even speak to me. She hung up on me before I could tell her the whole story."

"She's devastated. It's probably going to take a while for her to realize that what happened isn't your fault."

"If she ever does. At least, I'm not scheduled to work at the Roadrunner the rest of the week, so I'm not likely to see her at the gallery for a while. She keeps dropping in there unexpectedly even though we have her schedule covered by other members."

I talked to Brian for over an hour, and by the time we said good night, I was feeling a bit more hopeful that Pamela would forgive me for the part I'd played in Nate's arrest. Even if she did, I was afraid it might be a long road back for our friendship, but there was nothing I could do about it at the moment. It was too soon. I doubted that she'd answer the phone if I tried to call her.

With a sigh, I went to the kitchen, checked my stash of herbal tea, and selected a peach-flavored blend. I glanced at the clock and realized that Emma should have been home by now. She usually let me know if she was going somewhere after work, but I didn't remember her mentioning that she and Matt had a date. Perhaps they'd decided to go out at the last minute.

While Laddie settled himself at my feet and Mona Lisa decided to socialize by plopping herself on my lap, I tried to distract myself by watching a silly reality show on television. After the show ended, I turned off the television and picked up an art magazine I'd checked out from the library. I'd just started turning pages when I heard the garage door open, and I felt a little lighter. Even though my baby was twenty-one now, I felt better knowing she was safe and sound at home.

"Hi, Mom," she greeted me as she set her purse down on the end table next to the sofa. As soon as Emma sat down, Mona Lisa jumped off my lap and onto Emma's.

"Deserter," I muttered with a smile. Laddie sat up, leaned against my legs, and rested his head on my thigh. He basked in my attention as I petted him, all the while casting a wary eye on his feline roomie.

Emma rolled her eyes at our pets' "sibling rivalry."

"Um, Mom. I need to ask you something."

"Sure, Emma. By the way, I'm not planning on going anywhere tomorrow if you want to take the car to work."

"Thanks. That would be great, but it isn't what I wanted to ask you."

"OK."

"Could I stay here with you this fall? I don't want to go back to USC."

"You want to drop out?" I asked, shocked that Emma would consider leaving school.

"No! Not drop out. I'd like to transfer to Northern Arizona University."

"But why? I thought you loved USC."

"I do, but I love Matt more."

Chapter 21

Emma had been quiet about her relationship with Matt, and she'd certainly never indicated it was serious. My daughter wasn't a flighty person, though, and she'd never mentioned the word "love" when talking about past boyfriends, so I knew she meant what she said.

I reached over and gently squeezed her hand. "I didn't realize you and Matt were so serious. That's wonderful! Of course, I'd love to have you stay here. It's a bit of a commute, though. Isn't the campus in Flagstaff?"

"Yes, but we'll only have to be there two days a week, and I can take one of my classes online. Matt's gone as far as he can here at the community college. He's going to drive us, and we can both still work at the feed store the rest of the week. Dennis has always been really flexible about scheduling."

"I take it Dennis doesn't know about this yet."

"He knows Matt planned to go to NAU in the fall and arrange his schedule so that he could still work. Dennis just doesn't know I'll still be here, too, but Marla's moving soon, and I know he can give me the hours."

"OK. Maybe we could re-arrange the studio and turn half of it into a room for you."

"No, Mom. I'm fine with the hide-a-bed right here. It won't be for forever you know."

"Hmm." I could have gone on, but I thought it best to save that discussion for another time. Was the ringing in my ears the sound of wedding bells? One thing I knew for sure: my baby was all grown up.

I didn't know Matt very well, but Emma, Belle, and Dennis had nothing but good things to say about him, and he'd always been pleasant and polite to me whenever I saw him. I couldn't help thinking back to my own college days when Ned and I had started dating. After we married, I put aside my aspirations for a career in art to help Ned build his insurance business. Two children, twenty-five years of marriage, and one divorce later, here I was, starting over—well into starting over, anyway. What if I'd been able to see what was to come when Ned had asked me to marry him all those years ago? I realized it was pointless to speculate. I could only hope that Emma's future would be bright and that she'd always be as happy as she was now.

With my mind on Emma's unexpected announcement, I didn't dwell on Nate's arrest or Pamela's reaction, not until the following morning when their situations hit me head on.

Emma had left for work, taking my SUV, and I was painting when I was interrupted by tapping on the outside door of the studio. Laddie rushed to the door ahead of me. As soon as he saw Susan, he sat up on his haunches with his front paws curled under his chin waiting expectantly for her to pet him. She handed me two Coffee Klatsch cups so that she could oblige my eager dog.

"Mocha for you, latte for me," she said as I set them down beside my laptop on the desk and waited until Laddie calmed down.

"Thanks, Susan. What's the occasion?"

"I'm afraid you might feel like something stronger after you hear what I have to say, but since it's early, I figured the mocha would have to do."

"Uh, oh. What's wrong?"

"Dawn and I were holding down the fort at the gallery this morning when Pamela popped in. I assured her we had her hours covered and that she didn't need to be there, but you know Pamela. She had to see for herself I suppose. Anyway, she went to her office, but she didn't close the door. About ten minutes later, Nate showed up."

"Nate? But he's in jail."

"He *was* in jail. They released him this morning."

Stunned, I sank into my desk chair. "I can't believe it. He confessed to murdering Rich yesterday. How can he be out? Surely, he didn't get bail so soon."

"No, the police let him go. They're not charging him. When he asked me if Pamela was there, she heard him and ran into the gallery. As soon as she found out they'd released him, she was all happy and hugging him, but the reunion didn't last for long. Lieutenant Belmont came in a few minutes later with a couple of cops in uniform, and he arrested Pamela for Rich's murder!"

"Oh, no. Poor Pamela! I still can't believe it. This can't be happening."

Susan pulled my spare chair over beside the desk, sat down, and took a sip of her latte.

"There's more. When the lieutenant started to read Pamela her rights, Nate got up in his face and yelled at him. Belmont threatened to arrest him for interfering, and he settled down. The uniforms led Pamela out of the gallery in handcuffs. The last we saw, Nate followed them and told Pamela not to say anything, that he was on his way to their lawyer's office."

"I wonder what happened. Like I said, Nate confessed to the murder. I heard him myself."

"I know. He told us about it after they hauled off Pamela. He's really devastated that they arrested her. According to Nate, the only reason he confessed was that he was afraid Pamela would be arrested, and he was trying to protect her. I guess Belmont figured out he was lying after they did some checking this morning and found out he was doing an emergency plumbing job for one of his regular customers at the time of the murder. He wasn't even in the park Sunday afternoon."

I groaned. "I really got it wrong this time. I was the one who convinced the lieutenant that we should try to get Nate to confess. I was so sure he stabbed Rich."

Susan took a long sip of her latte and set the cup back down on my desk. "Nate said he didn't blame you, but I'm not sure Pamela feels the same."

"I know. She hung up on me last night when we were talking about it. I was wondering whether or not she'd ever speak to me again, and now she's been arrested herself—just what I'd hoped to avoid, not that I want an innocent man to end up in prison. I truly thought he'd done it. Obviously I was way off track with my reasoning, but I didn't think so at the time. Even Lieutenant Belmont bought into my theory."

"You're good at figuring this stuff out. I wouldn't have a clue where to begin myself, but you have a good track record, so don't give up now. Pamela needs you more than ever."

I put my elbows at my desk and rubbed my temples. I wondered where I'd gone wrong.

"I seem to be doing more harm than good," I moaned.

"This is no time to quit. Come on; get a grip," Susan urged.

"OK, you're right," I said, looking up at Susan. "There's just one teensy problem. When I talked Lieutenant Belmont into going along with my plan to try to get Nate to confess, he made me promise to 'stand down,' as he put it, if it didn't pan out."

"You can't be serious."

"Come to think about it, he actually asked me if I understood that I should 'stand down,' and I said that I did—understand, that is—so I guess I never technically promised to quit trying to find the killer if it wasn't Nate."

"Ah, ha. A loophole."

"Yep."

"Let me help," Susan exclaimed. "Just tell me what you need me to do."

I shot her a grateful look and nodded. "Well, I guess the first thing is to go back to square one and look farther afield. Obviously, I didn't consider all the possibilities when I pegged Nate as Rich's killer. What I knew pointed to Nate, but it was circumstantial at best. That's why I needed to get him to confess. There wasn't a shred of solid physical evidence against Nate, at least not as far as I knew."

"Why Nate? What made you suspect him?"

As I explained my former hypothesis to Susan, I realized now how flimsy my rationale had been. I couldn't help feeling guilty about accusing Nate of a crime he hadn't committed. I regretted my part in his misguided confession, which had served only to delay Pamela's arrest.

Now Pamela was in jail, facing the prospect of a trial and possibly a life sentence in prison if a jury convicted her. The police had stopped searching for the killer since they thought Pamela had done the deed, and Pamela's lawyer would be planning legal maneuvers to convince a jury to acquit her, rather than looking for her husband's killer.

"What next, Sherlock?" Susan asked.

We smiled wanly at each other, but our moment of levity was brief.

"Good question, Watson," I said. "Very good question."

Chapter 22

"We probably should try to find out more about Rich himself. Then we'll have more to go on." I said. "I didn't know him very well, but my impression of him was that he was something of a hothead. Remember how he acted at the Fourth of July party?"

"I got there late, so I didn't see the scuffle with his neighbor, but I heard about it," Susan said.

"Oh, that's right."

"I agree with you about his temperament. Chip's gone way out of his way to avoid both Rich and Pamela because of the guy's jealousy, not that it was *totally* unfounded, but Rich made a mountain out of a molehill. There was never anything serious between Pamela and Chip."

"I know. Rich wouldn't let it go. Mrs. Bramble told me Pamela and Rich had argued about Chip on more than one occasion. That reminds me: do we know exactly what happened to the painting Chip gave Pamela? Chip seemed to think that Rich destroyed it, but did anyone *see* him do it?"

"I don't know, but Pamela might. There's no way we're going to be able to ask her now, though. Nobody but her lawyer will be able to visit her, but I can check with Nate to find out whether her initial appearance in court has been scheduled yet."

"Good idea."

"Unfortunately, I know from bitter experience that it's supposed to happen within twenty-four hours. Thank goodness they decided not to charge me before I had to appear. I'll never forgive Belmont. It's his fault I spent a night in jail. Even though it's been over a year, I still have nightmares."

"I can imagine—what a terrible experience."

"It is for sure. I can't picture Pamela having to spend time in jail."

"Neither can I, but if we don't figure out who the real killer is, she could easily wind up in prison. That would be even more horrible than the local jail."

"Ugh." Susan shuddered. "We can't let that happen."

After we hashed Pamela's dilemma over for a few more minutes, Susan left. She was going to contact Nate to find out about Pamela's initial appearance and also ask some of the members of the Roadrunner who'd exhibited at Art in the Park or helped at the gallery's booth whether they knew anything about how the painting Chip had given Pamela had been slashed.

I planned to do some research to find out about Rich's business. I had only a dim idea about what he did for a living—something having to do with computer software, I thought. It was possible that his dealings had somehow led to his murder. Pamela had told me that he'd wanted to cut expenses in order to improve his balance sheet prior to taking out a loan. I wondered just how bad his financial situation had been, or whether it was bad at all. Perhaps he'd been using it as an excuse to get rid of Mrs. Bramble, although I had no idea why he'd want to do that.

I opened my laptop and searched for Rich's business website while I sipped my now-cold mocha. Despite its tepid temperature, the chocolatey coffee drink tasted good.

Because I didn't know the name of his business, I started my search with Rich's name. Not surprisingly, a ton of results popped up, so I quickly added "and Lonesome Valley" after "Richard Smith" in the search bar. By adding his address, I finally found him and learned that his middle name was Joseph, but there was no business listed in his name on the city's business license site. I figured that his company was probably registered as a corporation.

After scrolling through some more results from my prior search, I was unable to connect Rich with his business. I called Susan and asked her to try to find out its name when she talked to Nate. She'd left him a message, but he hadn't yet returned her call, so she was busy contacting gallery members to find out if anyone knew anything about the ripped painting Chip had given Pamela. She reported that she'd had no luck so far.

Drawing a blank about what my next move should be, I decided I needed to clear my head, so I called Laddie, and we went into the backyard for a game of fetch. By the time I was ready to call a halt to playtime, Laddie was panting but still wagging his tail.

"OK, one more, Laddie," I said as I tossed his hard rubber ball across the yard. He ran after it, swooped it up, and brought it back to me, obligingly dropping it at my feet. Ready for another round, he looked up at me expectantly.

"All right, but this time I really mean it."

I gently tossed the ball underhand, and Laddie leapt up and caught it in his mouth before it ever landed.

"Good job," I told him when he returned the ball to me. I plopped myself in a lawn chair on the patio while Laddie sat beside me, his chin in the air inviting me to stroke his neck.

"You never give up, do you, boy?" I said, as I ran my hand through his fur from his neck to his chest.

He answered by immediately pointing his nose in the air again. As I was petting him, I heard my cellphone ring. I'd left it on the desk in the studio, but the ringing stopped before we got there. Glancing at the caller's name, I frowned. I didn't recognize it, but, obviously, I'd put it in my contacts so I should know who it was. I scrolled through the list to find Jennifer Landis. As soon as I saw the note under her name, I recognized her as the woman who'd commissioned the pet portrait of her dog at Art in the Park. I couldn't believe I'd spaced my appointment with her, but now I remembered we'd arranged for me to meet her beagle Betsy.

"Uh, oh" I murmured to myself. "I forgot. I'm supposed to meet her today."

Jennifer answered on the first ring when I called her back. We arranged to meet at her house early in the afternoon, and she gave me her address. I took my digital camera out of the top drawer of my desk and replaced the old batteries. Although my phone probably would do an adequate job with the candid shots of Betsy that I planned to take, I knew the camera, which went through batteries almost as fast as I could snap photos, would be a better choice.

After I stowed the camera in my bag, I glanced down at the paint-spattered t-shirt I was wearing and resolved to remember to change it right after lunch. I went to my closet and selected a bright yellow gauze button-down shirt and hung it on the back of the door, ready to change into before I left for Jennifer's.

When it came time for me to leave the house, Laddie sensed that something was up as soon as I discarded my t-shirt and reached for the other top. Mona Lisa was nowhere to be seen, but Laddie didn't leave my side as I opened the door to the garage.

"Oops."

The garage was empty. I'd forgotten that Emma had taken my SUV to work. After I assured Laddie that I'd be back soon, I hastily called for an Uber and went to the curb to wait. Luckily, it didn't take long before the car arrived to whisk me away. Despite the short delay, I knocked on Jennifer's door right on the dot of one o'clock, just as we'd arranged, which pleased me because I didn't like to keep a client waiting, especially one who'd seemed a bit hesitant about allowing me to come to her house when I'd first mentioned it.

Betsy was right on Jennifer's heels as she opened the door, and as soon as she spotted me, the little beagle jumped up and put her front paws on my legs in a bid for attention.

"Hi, Betsy," I said, as I reached down to pet her.

"Betsy, stop that," Jennifer commanded, but the dog ignored her. "No," she insisted as she swooped down and gathered the wiggling beagle into her arms.

"I'm sorry," Jennifer apologized as I stepped inside, and she led me to her den in the back of the house. "Betsy gets so excited whenever we have company."

"No worries. My golden retriever's been known to do the same thing," I said, smiling.

"Would you like a cup of coffee?" Jennifer asked as I took a seat on a plush brown sofa.

"Sure, that would be nice. Just black is fine."

"Be right back."

Betsy followed Jennifer into the kitchen, but she didn't stay long. She back-tracked to me and jumped up on my lap. She was a lively little dog, and I hoped I'd be able to get some good pictures.

In a couple of minutes, Jennifer returned with a cup of coffee in a delicate china tea cup and set it, along with her own cup, on the coffee table in front of the sofa. Once she'd set the cups down, she coaxed Betsy into her arms and set her down on the floor.

"Sit, Betsy," she said, and Betsy sat.

"She knows her commands," Jennifer explained, "but she doesn't always follow them right away."

"Sounds familiar."

Betsy managed to maintain her position for a few minutes while we drank our coffee and I explained that I would take a few candid shots, both inside and outside, and that my painting wouldn't be a reproduction of any of photos but that I liked to use them for reference since they could give me a good idea of the dog's personality.

"OK, Betsy, go get a toy," Jennifer said, and the little beagle trotted over to a box in the corner that I hadn't noticed before and snatched a small rubber rabbit out of it before lying down and chewing on the bunny.

"Put your toy in the box," Jennifer told Betsy, and the little hound stood up, walked back to the toy box, and dropped the rabbit.

"That's a good one," I said, chuckling as I took a picture of her dropping the toy.

Betsy looked expectantly at Jennifer who signaled to the dog by patting her thigh that she was welcome on her lap. Happy to cuddle up with her pet parent, Betsy jumped up and settled herself while I took a few more pictures.

After a few minutes, I suggested that we go outside where Betsy raced around the small backyard, and I took a video of her. Then I had Jennifer hold Betsy while I snapped a few headshots.

Dropping my camera back into my bag, I nodded at Jennifer, and she released her pet who'd begun to wiggle.

"I think that'll do it," I said. "Betsy's a great subject. It'll be fun to paint her portrait."

"I can't wait to see it," she enthused. "About three weeks you said?"

"About that." I didn't want to commit myself to having the painting done sooner, especially since I wanted to spend some time investigating, but, of course, I didn't tell Jennifer that.

She walked with me back through the house to the entryway, and Betsy followed along beside us.

I reached into my bag for my keys and pulled them out. As Jennifer opened the front door, I noticed a group of framed photos on a side table. At first, I didn't recognize any of the people in the pictures except Jennifer, but for some reason I took a second look and gasped as I noticed a face I hadn't expected to see.

Chapter 23

"Looks like Hal Quinlan," I said, pointing to a picture of Jennifer and Hal with a group of people in the background.

"Yes, he's a friend of mine. I've known Hal forever," she said. "Our parents were members of the Lonesome Valley Country Club back when we were in high school, so we ran around with the same crowd. How do you know him?"

"I don't really. I recently met him at a Fourth of July party."

"The one given by the guy who was murdered, right?" Jennifer continued without waiting for me to affirm her assumption. "Hal told me about it. I don't like to speak ill of the dead, but he said the guy was a real jerk, and not just that night, either. Still, it was terrible—what happened to him. I wouldn't wish that on anyone."

Deciding it was probably better not to comment, I assured Jennifer that I'd let her know when I'd completed Betsy's portrait. I reached down and gave Betsy a pat before leaving.

As Jennifer closed the door, I walked down her porch steps and realized that, since I didn't have my car, I would feel awkward standing in front of Jennifer's house while I waited for an Uber to arrive. Often it could take a while in Lonesome Valley, so I walked to the corner before calling for a ride. I was glad I hadn't lingered outside Jennifer's house because fifteen minutes later, I was still waiting for a car to show up.

Just as I was contemplating walking the four miles home, I got an alert: the driver was on the way. I sighed with relief. It was a hot afternoon, and my sandals weren't exactly made for hiking.

It was another five minutes before the red Toyota Camry pulled up to the curb. I opened the door and sank gratefully into the back seat.

"Hey, Amanda!"

"Chip?"

"In the flesh. Don't be a stranger. You can sit in the front seat with me."

"I didn't recognize the car," I said as I climbed out of the back seat, opened the front passenger door, and slid into the front seat. "When did you start driving for Uber?"

"Just a few days ago, and the car's new—well, new to me anyway. My old car died, and there was no reviving it." He pulled out into the street. "I figured some extra cash would come in handy. I had to borrow money from my parents to buy this Toyota."

"Well, I'm glad you have wheels, anyway."

"Speaking of which, where are yours?"

"Oh, Emma took my SUV to work this morning. I would have dropped her off if I'd remembered I had an appointment with a client."

"The lady who commissioned the beagle portrait?"

"Yep, the same."

"Did I tell you I picked up a commission at Art in the Park, too?"

"No, you didn't say anything about it."

"Probably because it happened at the end of the day Sunday. I'm going to be painting a mural for the new day care center downtown. I guess the owner saw the wall I painted at the Coffee Klatsch."

"That's great, Chip."

"Yeah, I'd feel more enthusiastic if Rich hadn't been killed. It's hard to concentrate when Pamela's in jail. Aunt Susan told me what happened with Nate. I guess he was trying to help, but I think the cops were so anxious to pin Rich's murder on someone that all his fake confession did was speed up Pamela's arrest."

"You could be right. Lieutenant Belmont admitted that the chief was pressing for action. Did the lieutenant ever talk to you again, you know, about the slashed painting?"

"No, I haven't heard from him, and I hope I don't. I'd bet anything that Rich destroyed it, though. I mean who else would have any reason to do something so mean? He knew I'd painted it. I saw Pamela put it away, under the table in the Roadrunner booth, after I gave it to her, probably so Rich wouldn't see it, but he must have found out."

"Wouldn't he have noticed it after she took it home, though? What was the point of hiding it?"

"I don't know. Maybe she was going to hang it in her office at the gallery, but I guess that doesn't make sense, either, because Rich comes in there to see her all the time."

"Right, but I think you're onto something. If she hung it in the meeting room, he would never have known you gave it to her. He knew you painted it because he watched your demo, but it wouldn't be unusual for a member's painting to be in the meeting room."

"He watched my demo, all right. He heckled me most of the way through it. Rich really wasn't a very nice man. I mean I can understand he had some reason to feel jealous of Pamela and me, although it wasn't really serious between us, but he never let up on her. You know me: I can't help flirting, but that's all it was."

From my own experience with Chip, I did know. I just hoped that Pamela's brief infatuation with Chip hadn't factored into Rich's murder.

"Home, sweet home," I said as Chip turned onto Canyon Drive. He stopped in front of my house, and I hopped out of the car. "Good luck with your new job!" I said.

"And good luck to you in finding out who really murdered Rich."

"Thanks, Chip. I have a feeling I'll need all the luck I can get."

"Aunt Susan told me you two are on the case. I'd like to help. Just tell me what I can do."

"I wish I knew. So far, we seem to be spinning our wheels. I really thought Nate was the culprit."

"Well, it can't be Pamela. There's no way. Just because. . . uh, I need to get going. Another passenger to pick up."

As I watched the red Camry pull away from the curb, I wondered what Chip had been about to tell me. I shrugged. It must not have been too important or he wouldn't have rushed off so fast to his next job.

Although I'd been gone less than two hours, Laddie greeted me as though he hadn't seen me for months. Mona Lisa was nowhere in sight. Evidently, whether I was home or not was a matter of supreme indifference to my calico kitty unless it was mealtime. When Laddie finally calmed down, I peeked over the back of the sofa and saw Mona Lisa curled up in one of her favorite hiding places. She looked up at me for a few seconds, yawned, and then, without changing position, returned to her nap, putting her head back down on her paws.

My next task would be to upload the pictures I'd taken of Betsy from my camera onto my laptop and do some preliminary sketching of the little hound, but before I did that, I took Laddie outside, into the backyard, for round two of playtime. As he raced around the yard, chasing his ball, I thought about poor Pamela, stuck in the jail. There was still no word from Susan, which meant she hadn't yet succeeded in contacting Nate.

Panting, Laddie returned to the patio. We went back inside, where it was much cooler, and I transferred Betsy's images to my laptop. I reviewed the pictures before picking up a sketch pad and playing around with different poses. I wasn't quite satisfied with my first couple of efforts, but the third sketch seemed to be shaping up the way I'd envisioned it. I liked to have a plan before starting on a commissioned pet portrait.

Satisfied that this one was coming along nicely, I decided to take a short break. I wouldn't be starting the actual painting until the next day, especially because I felt my energy level ebbing. In fact, as soon as I stood up and stretched, I realized that I felt quite drained. Intending to rest for just a few minutes, I lay down on the sofa with Laddie on the floor beside me and closed my eyes.

The next thing I knew I was rudely awakened by my cellphone. Groaning, I rolled off the sofa and picked it up. As soon as I saw the number on my phone's display, my eyes widened. I wasn't likely to forget it: that number had been on our business cards for years. Even though Ned had moved his insurance office a couple of times since starting the business right after we graduated from college, the phone number had always remained the same.

"Ned. What's wrong?" I hadn't talked to my ex-husband in over a year. I couldn't imagine why he'd be calling me now—not unless it was an emergency.

"I'll tell you what's wrong. Emma's changing schools; that's what."

"Oh," I said, breathing a sigh of relief.

"That's *all* you have to say? You put her up to it, didn't you?"

"Don't be ridiculous. I didn't know anything about her plans to transfer to NAU until last night when she told me she wanted to stay here."

"And that's another thing. You barely have room for yourself in that tiny little dump of yours, and you want *my* daughter to live there."

"She's my daughter, too, and she wants to stay here. It will mean a big savings on room and board. I don't understand why you're so upset."

"Emma never wants to visit me, and when she does, she barely speaks to me. I wouldn't even have known she wasn't going back to USC if Dustin hadn't told me. I don't know what you've been up to, but you've turned my own daughter against me!"

"You did that yourself, Ned."

Tears sprang to my eyes as I thought about the break-up of our family. Although I loved my new life and thought I was over the divorce, I knew Emma wasn't. It didn't help that Ned's new wife Candy was only a couple of years older than Emma or that they'd had a baby before the ink was dry on our divorce papers or that Emma's bedroom had been turned into a nursery for their son.

Ned had behaved cavalierly about the entire situation. I didn't think he'd made any real effort to help Emma reconcile herself to the new family dynamics.

"Oh, sure. Blame me!" he yelled.

I decided I didn't need to listen to more of his ranting. Emma was an adult, and she could make her own decisions. She didn't need her father's approval. "I do blame you, Ned, but, believe it or not, I want you and Emma to have a good relationship. I'm afraid you're going to have to work it out with her yourself, though. This is between the two of you. I'm going to hang up now because we're not getting anywhere."

I poked my phone to disconnect the call, and then, for good measure, I turned it off. I'd had about enough of my ex-husband for one day. If he called again, I wasn't sure I'd answer the phone.

Sighing, I rubbed my temples. Laddie came over, cocking his head at me, and Mona Lisa crept out from her hiding place and rubbed against my legs. I stooped down and gave them both a hug.

"OK, gang, I shouldn't let Ned upset me." Of course, I was talking to myself, but my pets acted as though they understood. At least, I liked to think so as they both snuggled closer to me.

Chapter 24

Still in cuddle mode, we moved to the sofa where Mona Lisa settled herself on my lap and Laddie sat beside me with his head resting on my lap. When Emma returned home from work, we were still sitting there.

Mona Lisa jumped down and ran to Emma, who picked her up. Mona Lisa wiggled, stretched, and draped herself around my daughter's neck while Laddie looked on but stayed beside me.

"What's wrong, Mom?" Emma asked. "You look kind of down."

"I guess I am. The cops found out Nate has an alibi so they let him go, and they've arrested Pamela. And one more thing—your father called. Evidently, he's not too happy with your decision to change schools."

"But I didn't tell him about that yet."

"I guess Dustin must have mentioned it."

"Oh, right. Well, it's not exactly a secret, and I really don't know why he'd care one way or another."

"He thinks I've turned you against him."

"That's not true! I can't help it if I don't like what he did. My darling stepmother's only a couple years older than me. Ewww!"

"I know it's a cliché, but what's done is done. We can't go back, and he *is* your father. I hope you can find some way to maintain a relationship with him."

"I suppose I could make more of an effort, but it just makes me so mad. They didn't need to turn my room into the nursery. The guest room's right across the hall from their bedroom, and it's way bigger than my room. Candy's happy enough to have me babysit so she and Dad can go out, but, otherwise, she doesn't want me around, and the feeling's mutual. I can't stand her, either!"

"I know it's hard, honey. I'm so sorry."

"Mom, there's nothing for *you* to feel sorry about, and Dad can like it or lump it as far as my transferring to NAU goes. It's my decision, not his. He ignores me most of the time, anyway. I don't know why he'd care."

"He probably realizes his little girl is slipping away."

"Well, news flash! I'm not his little girl anymore, and he can't tell me what to do!"

I was regretting telling Emma about Ned's phone call since his objection to her transferring to NAU had raked up ongoing grievances. Emma had never forgiven Ned for our divorce, and I couldn't really blame her for her feelings toward Candy. I hadn't liked Candy from the moment she'd come into the insurance office to apply for office assistant, but, despite my objections, Ned had hired her. At the time the idea had been that she'd replace me in the insurance office so that I could concentrate on my painting after years of working in Ned's business. Candy had not only succeeded in replacing me in the office, although she no longer worked there since she'd become Mrs. Ned Trent, but in replacing me as Ned's wife, too.

Unfortunately, although Emma, Dustin, and I had all been hurt by Ned's decision to throw me over for another woman, Emma was having the most difficult time dealing with our changed family dynamics. I was happy in my new life as a full-time artist, and Dustin, who had a good job and his own apartment in Kansas City, had adjusted to the change better than Emma.

Since I could tell that Emma wasn't in any mood for a reconciliation call with Ned, I changed the subject and suggested that we go out to dinner.

Emma brightened right away. The two of us didn't dine out together very often, so it would be a fun little break from eating at home.

"How about that little Greek restaurant downtown?" Emma asked.

"Sounds good to me. Let me just give Laddie and Mona Lisa their dinners, and we'll be off."

A few minutes later, the pets were still chowing down when we quietly exited through the kitchen door.

When we arrived at the restaurant, it wasn't very busy yet, and we had our choice of tables. We picked a quiet corner spot where we could look out on Main Street while we had dinner. Emma and I both decided on salads, rather than a heavier meal. Our server appeared quickly, took our orders, and returned with our drinks.

She had just set my iced tea down when my cellphone rang. As soon as I saw it was Susan calling, I answered.

"Any news?"

"Yes, finally. I just connected with Nate, and he told me that Pamela's initial appearance is tomorrow morning. Her lawyer is hoping to get her out on bail, although he said that wasn't very likely to happen. Nate promised to let me know, though. By the way, he said to tell you he isn't mad at you; he knows you were trying to help Pamela."

"I was, but I'm sure she isn't too happy with me right at the moment."

"She'll get over it. She *has* to. If you ask me, you're her best chance of staying out of prison."

"I don't know about that. Look at what I've already done," I moaned.

"Stop that! Come on, Amanda. Quit beating yourself up over suspecting Nate. The cops bought into your theory, too, remember?"

"Yes, you're right. OK, I'm going to get a grip. Did you get a chance to ask any of the Roadrunner's members whether they saw Chip's painting after he gave it to Pamela?"

"I talked to most of them who were at Art in the Park, and nobody saw anything. None of them knew that Chip had given Pamela his demo painting, either."

"Hmm. Well, I guess that's a dead end, but we had to check. Thanks for calling everybody. Unfortunately, I didn't get very far, either. I tried to find out about Rich's business, but I couldn't even come up with its name. I guess we'll have to ask Nate about that. Surely, he'd know."

"I imagine so."

"All right. I'll check with him when I get home." When I told Susan that Emma and I were dining at the Greek restaurant downtown, she suggested that we have the pistachio baklava for dessert.

"Would you like to try the baklava?" I asked Emma after Susan and I finished our call. "Susan says it's the best."

"Sure, but let's get it to go, if it's all right with you. Matt gets off work at eight, and we may go to a movie."

"All right."

After we finished our salads and our server approached us with the dessert menu, I ordered the pistachio baklava to go. We waited quite a while for our take-out dessert, and I could see that Emma was starting to get a bit antsy, so I was relieved when a different server dropped off our to-go box at our table along with the bill.

Emma picked up the check and volunteered to pay, but I knew she was on a tight budget, and it had been my idea to go out for dinner, anyway.

"It's my treat, Emma."

"Thanks, Mom," she said, grinning as she handed over the bill. "My salad was really good. I bet the baklava will be, too."

We didn't have to wait for the server to show up again to pay the bill since the restaurant had a cash register up front, where customers paid. As soon as we got into the car, Emma pulled out her cellphone to check the time.

"It looks like Matt already called me. I better call him back."

My mind wandered as Emma and Matt chatted and made their plans for the evening. I decided to call Nate when I got home, rather than waiting until tomorrow. I hoped he'd be able to tell me something about Rich's business, even though I felt reluctant to talk with him. After all, the last time I'd seen him, the police were leading him away from my house in handcuffs. Even though Susan had assured me that Nate didn't blame me for his arrest, I couldn't help feeling uneasy.

I felt even more nervous when I saw that Nate's plumbing van was parked in front of my house. I pulled into the garage and went out front while Emma went inside. Nate was sitting in the van's driver's seat, but he evidently hadn't spotted me. He didn't look as though he were moving, and I noticed his mouth was open. I had a sickening feeling as I crept around the back of the van and peered in the open window.

Suddenly, Nate jerked awake. Startled, I jumped back. I must have screamed because Nate looked at me in confusion.

"Are you OK?" he asked.

"Yes, sorry; are you?"

"Sure, guess I must have fallen asleep while I was waiting. I wanted to talk with you. Pamela needs your help."

"So you're not mad at me?"

"Not anymore. It was as much my fault as yours. I realized you must have really thought I killed Rich, and so did the cops, or they wouldn't have arrested me."

"I'm sorry, Nate. Truly. We need to figure out who the real culprit is, and the sooner the better."

"I couldn't agree more. That's why I'm here. I was hoping you'd be willing to keep investigating because there's no way my sister had anything to do with the death of her husband."

"Right. I'll do what I can. Up to now, I obviously haven't gotten very far."

Nate put his hand over his mouth to cover a yawn.

"Sorry, Amanda. I'm really tired."

"Why don't you come on in the house, and I'll make us some coffee. I was going to call you tomorrow to check on a couple of things, anyway. We might as well talk now."

"Sure."

Nate jumped out of his van and followed me inside where Laddie greeted us both.

"Regular or decaf?" I asked. Although I knew Nate must be exhausted, he seemed to want to stay awake for a while.

"I guess I'd better go with the decaf. And just black will be fine. I won't be much good to Pamela or anyone else if I don't get some sleep tonight."

Nate sank onto the sofa while I brewed the coffee and Laddie kept me company. Mona Lisa was nowhere to be seen. I could hear Emma rattling the hangers in my closet, probably trying to decide what to wear for her date. I suspected Mona Lisa was camped out on my bed where she could keep an eye on Emma.

"Here you are, Nate." I set a mug of coffee on the side table next to him. He picked up the cup, took a sip, and leaned back.

"It wasn't the first time I ever spent a night in jail," Nate said, "but it was the noisiest."

He glanced at me, and I suppose I must have looked surprised at his admission, but he just laughed.

"I assume you must have heard about my checkered past."

"Well. . . ."

"It's OK. I got into a lot of trouble when I was younger. Bar fights and such. I have a terrible temper when I get riled, but I've learned to tamp it down over the years."

Despite Mrs. Bramble's opinion of Pamela's brother, I tended to believe Nate.

"Mom, could I see you for a second?" Emma called from the hallway. "I can't decide which top to wear."

"Excuse me for a moment, Nate."

I joined my daughter in the bedroom, and she quietly closed the door.

"Mom, what are you doing?" Emma whispered. "Why is *he* here?"

"I need to ask him about Rich's business."

"I don't think that's a good idea. It's not safe."

"It's all right, Emma. He's not angry with me."

"How can you be sure? Matt'll be here any time, and I think we better stay home until Nate leaves."

"Emma, there's no need. I'll be fine. You and Matt go and enjoy the movie, just like you planned."

"I don't know," Emma said reluctantly.

I opened the bedroom door and told Emma I thought she should wear the turquoise blue top in a voice loud enough for Nate to hear me before re-joining him in the living room.

"Sorry, Nate. Fashion emergency."

He smiled. "I wouldn't know anything about that."

"Well, let me ask you about something you *do* know."

"Shoot."

"What's the name of Rich's company? I couldn't find any enterprises listed under his name in Lonesome Valley."

Nate didn't answer right away, and I thought maybe he was trying to remember the name. Meanwhile, Emma came out of the bedroom and told me Matt was on his way up the hill and she'd meet him outside, but before she left, she gave Nate a sideways glance, leaned toward me, and whispered for me to be careful. I squeezed her hand and stood at the door watching as Matt drove up, got out of the car, and opened the passenger door for Emma, but not before he gave her a big hug and kiss.

"Sorry, Nate," I said, returning to the chair where I'd been sitting.

"That's OK. Let me think. Something to do with software? I must have heard it sometime, but Rich never talked about business with me or much of anything else for that matter. He barely tolerated me at family gatherings."

"Could you find out from Pamela? I'm not sure she's even speaking to me at this point."

"Sure, I can ask her, but it might be a while before she can have visitors if she doesn't get bail tomorrow. I'm hoping she will, but her lawyer says the chances are slim."

"Is there anyone else you can think of that might have had it in for Rich?"

"That guy who lives next door."

"Hal Quinlan?"

"Yeah, the one who jumped over the wall during the Fourth of July party. He and Rich were always feuding about something; they've sued each other more than once, always over petty stuff. Pamela tried to referee to keep peace in the neighborhood, but it was kind of a lost cause."

"I considered him, of course, but he was in Las Vegas the afternoon Rich was killed. He couldn't have made it back here in time to stab him."

"Yeah, well, I didn't really think he did it. Problem is nobody really stands out. I guess that's why the cops zoomed in on Pamela, just because she's the wife. I don't get it, though. What's her motive supposed to be? I may not have cared for my brother-in-law, but she was crazy about the guy."

"Good question, but I don't have the answer."

"I should get going. I've got a full day tomorrow at work, and I need to take some time off in the morning to go to Pamela's initial appearance." Nate stood, and Laddie jumped up and followed us to the front door. "Thanks for the coffee, Amanda. I'll let you know what happens in court tomorrow."

Nate patted Laddie on the head, and I watched for a few seconds as Nate walked to his van. There was a car parked behind the van, and I immediately realized whose.

As soon as Nate pulled away from the curb, I told Laddie to stay, closed the door enough so that he couldn't come outside, and called to Emma. When I went over to the car, I could see Matt in the driver's seat.

"Why haven't you left for the movie yet?" I asked.

"And leave you alone with Nate? No way," my daughter replied.

"Hi, Ms. Trent," Matt said sheepishly. "Emma was worried, so we thought we'd hang around and make sure everything was all right."

I shook my head and smiled. I couldn't very well be angry at my daughter for wanting to protect me.

"OK, then, you'd better be on your way, or you'll miss the movie."

"'Bye, Mom, and don't forget to lock the door!"

Chapter 25

The next morning I worked on the pet portrait of Betsy while I waited to hear some news from Nate or Susan about what happened at Pamela's court appearance.

The call didn't come until almost noon.

Nate sounded very relieved as he told me that Pamela would be able to be released on bond. He wasn't quite so happy about the size of the bond, though—a cool million dollars!—but he explained that only ten percent would be required by the bonding company that would put up the bail money. According to Nate, Pamela could easily raise the money. I held off suggesting that I'd like to visit her as soon as she went home, both because I figured she'd be in no mood to see me and also because I knew she'd be exhausted and need some rest.

"Could you arrange for me to come to see Pamela at home tomorrow?" I asked.

"Sure thing. I'll call you back later. I have to get to a job now, but Pamela's lawyer will let me know when I can pick her up."

I felt I was pretty much at a standstill until Pamela and I could get together, so after a quick lunch and a session of fetch with Laddie in the backyard, I returned to the studio to work on my painting. Three hours later, I had made good progress and decided to stop work for the day. It was too hot to take Laddie for another walk, so I did some laundry and a few household chores. I'd just finished dusting when Susan called.

"Nate's beside himself," she told me. "Pamela wanted to put her house up as collateral for the bail bond company, but her lawyer found out it's mortgaged to the hilt. There's hardly any equity there, although Pamela doesn't know it yet. Last I heard, Nate was going to put his own house up so that she can get out of jail today."

"Something's not right. You'd think Pamela would know about the mortgage situation."

"Unless Rich did something sneaky, like put a second mortgage on it without telling her. Could he have tricked her into signing the documents somehow?"

"Maybe. I'm getting the feeling his financial situation might have had something to do with his death."

"I know. Remember that he wanted to fire Mrs. Bramble just to save money? That seemed odd to me."

"We're going to have to dig deeper, and I don't know how much help Pamela will be. It sounds as though Rich kept her in the dark about finances. It's a good thing she has Nate looking out for her. I guess I had him pegged all wrong. He's certainly acting like a good brother."

"I agree. It's too bad he has to put up his house, but I sure hope he can get Pamela bailed out today. It would be awful if she had to spend another night in that horrible jail."

"Yes, it would. Poor Pamela! She's lost her husband, been charged with his murder, and now she's going to find out about the mortgage on their house. Last year, right after I bought my house, I mentioned to her that I had been fortunate to be able to pay for it so I don't have a mortgage, and she told me that she and Rich were looking forward to paying off their mortgage very soon."

"The mortgage problem may be the least of her worries if she's convicted of homicide."

"I just don't see that they have much of a case against her. Even though the knife came from her kitchen, lots of people had access to it, especially the night of the Fourth of July party."

"That's for sure."

"I kind of wonder whether Rich took the knife himself. You know—to cut up the painting Chip gave Pamela."

"Oh, wow. That's possible."

"As far as the blood on her hands and clothes, it's easily explained since Pamela was the one who found Rich first."

"Right, and she had no reason to want him dead."

"Exactly. Couples argue all the time. I think the cops are exaggerating the argument they had that Sunday morning. Supposedly, Rich wanted to fire Mrs. Bramble, and Pamela didn't. That's no reason for Pamela to kill Rich."

"The district attorney will probably say that they got into another argument, and she stabbed him in the heat of the moment."

"That's pure speculation. The case against her isn't only circumstantial; it's also really thin, if you ask me. Oh, another call. I better take it. Looks like it's Nate."

"Later," Susan said and hung up.

"Nate, what happened?" I was so eager to hear the latest news, I didn't even say hello.

"I wanted to let you know that I'll be able to pick up Pamela in about an hour. The bond's been posted." Nate sounded weary.

"Finally, some good news."

"Good and bad. I'm glad she's going to get out of jail, but I have a feeling Rich was up to something. Pamela thought their house was almost paid off, but Pamela's lawyer learned she has almost no equity. If she had to sell it, the proceeds wouldn't be enough to pay the real estate commission. I'm afraid to find out what condition Rich's business was in; I'm guessing not very good. I'm worried about how we're going to afford her lawyer, but I don't want her to have to depend of a public defender when her life's at stake. I make a decent living, but I don't have much savings, and now that I've put my house up as collateral for the bonding company, I doubt that I can take out a second mortgage on it."

"Nate, I'm so sorry. I know all this comes as a huge shock. Everybody thought Rich's business was doing well. I can't remember Pamela ever expressing any concern over finances."

"I can't, either. I think she was totally in the dark about whatever Rich was doing."

"We have to find out," I said. "Maybe Pamela didn't involve herself in Rich's business, but we can at least get a lead on its financial condition by talking to some of the employees. Right at the moment, we don't even know the name of his company, and I think we'll need Pamela's consent to look into it. Can you arrange for me to see her tomorrow morning?"

"I'm going to insist on it. Make it nine o'clock unless you hear from me otherwise."

"I'll be there."

"Thanks, Amanda. I really appreciate your help."

"I'll do my best, but I admit that I'm stumped right at the moment. Will you be at Pamela's in the morning?"

"Nope. I have to work. I'm already running behind schedule. I had to postpone a couple of jobs today, and some of my customers really can't wait any longer."

I could understand Nate's dilemma with the amount of pressure he was under to help his sister and keep his own business afloat. Defending Pamela on a homicide charge would be frightfully expensive. Now, I felt even guiltier about having suspected him in the first place.

There really wasn't much I could do until I could talk to Pamela. I decided to try to get my mind off her case for a while and start fresh in the morning.

Emma would be coming home from work soon. I hadn't given dinner a thought, so I rummaged around in the refrigerator, trying to get some inspiration. I settled on a quick pasta dish and melon.

The cantaloupe that I'd picked up at the grocery store a few days earlier should be at its peak ripeness now. I cut it in half, scooped out the seeds, and used my melon baller to scoop out the flesh into perfect little balls. I set them in the refrigerator to chill and texted Emma to find out if she would be leaving work on time. As soon as she confirmed that she was leaving the feed store, I put the pasta on to boil.

I was draining it when she came in the door, and Mona Lisa and Laddie rushed to her. Mona Lisa meowed loudly until Emma picked her up while she managed to pet Laddie at the same time.

"It's nice to be wanted," she laughed as the pets snuggled closer.

"If you can pacify them for about five minutes, dinner will be ready. Theirs, too."

Emma inched her way to the sofa and sat down, still holding Mona Lisa, while Laddie crowded close to her. After she settled herself, my golden boy sat down next to her and put his head on her lap. As she stroked him, Mona Lisa took a swipe at him, but Emma fended her off, and the jealous cat climbed on Emma's shoulder, regarding Laddie with disdain from her new perch. Laddie gave Mona Lisa a ha-ha-ha look and continued to bask in her attention.

Meanwhile, I finished preparing dinner for us and our pets, neither of whom wasted any time running to the kitchen as soon as they heard me set their bowls down at opposite ends of the cramped space.

Emma and I had just sat down to eat our own meals when her cellphone rang. She glanced at it and looked at me in distress.

"It's Dad," she groaned. "I don't really feel like getting into it with him right now."

A few seconds after she poked the phone to decline the call, my cellphone rang. Sure enough, it was Ned.

"It's your father," I told Emma.

Chapter 26

She groaned. "OK, don't answer. I'm going to call him back and get it over with. I suppose there's no point in trying to avoid him."

Emma had barely touched her food, so I wrapped her plate with foil and set it in the refrigerator for later as she went into the bedroom and closed the door. It wasn't long before I heard her raise her voice, and Laddie began to whimper softly at the sound.

I didn't feel much like eating now, so I put my plate in the refrigerator, too, and took Laddie outside. Luckily, Mona Lisa didn't seem to feel the need to be comforted. She'd snuggled up on the top rung of her kitty tree as soon as she finished dinner, and she was already sound asleep when Laddie and I stepped onto the back patio.

Even though the windows were closed because the air conditioning was on, I could still hear Emma every once in a while. I tried to distract myself by playing fetch with Laddie, but I couldn't help feeling angry with Ned for giving Emma a hard time. Much as I hoped to stay out of their feud, I felt as though I were right in the middle of it. I didn't relish the thought of playing referee, and I certainly wasn't going to try to convince Emma to return to California to finish her degree, although I knew that's exactly what Ned wanted me to do.

After about ten minutes, I didn't hear any more shouting, so I called Laddie, and we went back inside. I found Emma on the sofa sobbing. With Laddie at my side, I rushed to her and put my arm around her while Laddie sat sandwiched between us and put his paw on Emma's knee. She couldn't help giggling at the dog's antics, and she wiped her eyes.

"I'm OK, Mom," she sniffed. "I don't know why I let Dad get to me like that. He can be so unreasonable sometimes."

"Did you happen to tell him about Matt?"

"Yes, but that only made him madder. He said I shouldn't change schools just to be with a boy. Can you believe he called Matt a 'boy'? He's twenty-eight years old! That's six years older than Dad was when you two got married."

Married? Hmm. Somehow, I wasn't surprised that Emma had used the "m" word. She wouldn't have considered changing schools to be near Matt if she weren't in love with him. I wondered just how far their plans had progressed. Had he already proposed?

"Emma, are you engaged?"

"Not officially, but we've talked about getting married. You're not going to try to talk me out of it, are you?"

"No. It's your decision. I don't know Matt very well, but from everything I've observed about him so far, he seems like a great guy."

"So you approve?"

"Of course. I approve of anybody who makes you happy. I would like to get to know him better. How about a barbecue tomorrow evening? Brian should be calling pretty soon. I'll check with him, but I'm sure he won't mind helping with the grill."

"Oh, Mom, I'd like to, but we already have tickets for the new play at the little theater for Saturday."

"Oh, well, we can do it another time. Maybe next Saturday?"

"That should be good. I'll check with Matt."

Later I found out my plan wouldn't have worked anyway. Brian had called to let me know that his corporate office was sending a team for a surprise site inspection over the weekend, so he'd be stuck at work and wouldn't be able to come home. It was the first time since he'd taken on his new job in southern Arizona that he hadn't been able to come home to Lonesome Valley for the weekend. With Brian absent, Emma and Matt occupied, and Belle and Dennis away in Michigan on vacation, it looked as though I'd have plenty of time on my hands.

I hoped Susan and I would be able to make some progress in our investigation. Although I wasn't exactly looking forward to seeing Pamela because I knew she was unhappy with me, I really needed her input if we were going to figure out who had murdered Rich.

I shouldn't have worried, though. Luckily, when I arrived at Pamela's the next morning, she'd had a change of heart, and I guessed I had Nate to thank for that.

Although I'd been expecting Mrs. Bramble to answer the door, Pamela opened it herself.

"Come in, Amanda," she said softly. "Let's go back to the den. Mrs. Bramble is making coffee."

The aroma of freshly brewed coffee mingled with vanilla and cinnamon wafted our way from the kitchen. The moment we sat down, Mrs. Bramble appeared with a tray, bearing coffee and coffee cake.

"The coffee cake smells divine," I said to Mrs. Bramble.

"I think you'll like it," she said proudly. "It's my latest recipe."

I took a bite, savoring its gooey texture and rich flavor. "Delicious!"

"Glad you like it," she said before returning to the kitchen.

Pamela sipped her coffee and looked at me sheepishly. "I want to apologize for the way I spoke to you on the phone. I was upset about Nate's arrest, but that's no excuse. I understand that you were only trying to help, but I know my brother, and he's no killer. Neither am I."

"Well, I certainly got it wrong, but I'd really like to get it right this time. We don't want you locked up for a crime you didn't commit. I suspect that Lieutenant Belmont doesn't think you did it, either, but the chief insisted on an arrest."

"Perhaps. The lieutenant never acted nasty toward me, the way he did to Susan. In fact, he's always been quite polite, even considerate. When they arrested me, I was in handcuffs, and they took me into a room to question me. The cop who brought me in wanted to attach the handcuffs to the table, but the lieutenant told him to take them off. Of course, my lawyer had told me not to say a word about the case, so as soon as he asked a question, I told him I wanted my lawyer there."

"That's odd since he already knew you had representation."

"I got the feeling he was just going through the motions. As soon as I mentioned my lawyer, the lieutenant said we'd wait until he arrived. Then he brought me a bottle of water and asked whether I wanted anything to eat."

"Strange. Lieutenant Belmont's usually so grumpy, but I'm glad he didn't act that way toward you. If I could just uncover some new evidence, maybe I could convince him to look into it because I have the distinct feeling that he doesn't think you should have been arrested."

What I didn't say was that I wasn't at all sure the lieutenant would pay any attention to me, not after the fiasco of Nate's arrest at my house. Then, too, there was the little matter that he'd told me he expected me to "stand down" if I was wrong about Nate. Of course, I felt I couldn't do that, not with Pamela's life hanging in the balance.

"I've been wondering if Rich's death could somehow be related to his business."

"I don't see how," Pamela said.

"I don't either, but we have to consider all the possibilities, and I don't really know anything about his business, not even its name."

"He used his own name. It's R. J. Smith Software."

"I couldn't find any business license in his name here in Lonesome Valley."

"It's based in Phoenix. Remember that he used to spend most of his time there?"

Although Pamela asked the question, she didn't pause for an answer. I did remember because it was during that time Pamela and Chip had their fling. I'd always thought Pamela's loneliness accounted for her paying attention to Chip's outrageous flirting.

"I guess he got tired of hearing me complain about his being gone so much that he decided to work from home. He still maintained the office in Phoenix and held occasional meetings there, but he was able to do pretty much everything else remotely."

"Did he mention any problems at work recently?"

"Well, yes," Pamela lowered her voice and glanced toward the kitchen. "I told you this a few days ago. He wanted to lay off Mrs. Bramble to save money because he said he needed to improve his balance sheet," she whispered.

"Right, you mentioned that he wanted to take out a loan, but do you know what he intended to do with the money? Was there some problem with the business, or was he planning on expanding perhaps?"

Pamela put her hand over her mouth and squinted. "I hate to admit it, Amanda, but he seldom discussed business with me, so I really know almost nothing about it. I have no idea why he needed the money, but I do know how we can find out."

Chapter 27

"I'll get in touch with Fred Wagner. He's the money guy at Rich's company. Officially, he's the vice-president and the controller. If anyone knows what Rich had in mind, it's Fred. A couple of days ago, he called, wanting to talk business, but I just wasn't up to it, so we agreed to meet after Rich's memorial service. I don't know when that will be yet. The coroner hasn't released Rich's body."

Tears began rolling down Pamela's cheeks. I rushed to sit beside her and put my arm around her, as she sobbed on my shoulder. I wished I hadn't had to involve her in my investigation, but there hadn't been any alternative since Nate wasn't able to help with any information about Rich's business dealings.

After a minute or so, Pamela took a paper napkin from the tray Mrs. Bramble had brought in earlier and dabbed her tears.

"Sorry, Amanda."

"There's nothing for you to be sorry about, Pamela."

"I still can't believe he's no longer with us. Sometimes, I think I hear his footsteps in the house after Mrs. Bramble's gone home for the day. You must think I'm crazy."

"Not at all, Pamela. You've suffered a huge loss."

She sniffed and wiped her eyes again. "I know. I can't seem to stop crying."

"Don't try. You need to let it out. It doesn't do any good to keep your feelings all bottled up inside."

"I know; you're right, but what am I going to do?" she wailed. "I miss him so much."

"Of course you do."

"I don't even know when I can have his memorial service. I guess I already told you that, though. I must be losing it."

"Pamela, don't worry about it. You have plenty to deal with."

"And the gallery. I should go in today, shouldn't I?"

"That's not necessary. The gallery will be fine. Ralph's keeping an eye on things, and he's making sure it's running smoothly."

With a trembling hand, Pamela picked up her cup, leaving the saucer on the tray. Her coffee was surely cold by now, but she took a sip anyway. She was about to set it back when it slipped out of her hand, dropping onto its saucer and shattering both pieces of china.

She gave a little cry and started sobbing again.

"I'll get it, Pamela."

I retrieved a piece of the broken cup that had bounced onto the floor and set it back on the tray. I checked the carpet for any other shards, but I didn't find any, so I picked up the tray and carried it into the kitchen.

Her back to me, Mrs. Bramble was standing at the sink and the water was running. Evidently she didn't hear me come in because she jumped when I set the tray down on top of the island counter.

"Oh!" she exclaimed, turning around.

"Pamela's pretty shaky," I told her. "She dropped her cup."

Mrs. Bramble looked at the remains of the porcelain cup and saucer and shook her head. "Too bad," she murmured. She picked up the broken pieces of china, put them in a paper bag, and deposited them in her recycle bin.

"She's so upset I can't talk to her now, but I think I'd better wait until she calms down."

"Poor Pamela. I don't know what to do for her."

"Just keep the household running, as you have been, I suppose. Nobody can make her feel any better. Right now, she's not thinking about it, but she could end up in prison if we can't figure out who killed Rich."

Mrs. Bramble nodded.

"I need information, but only if it's valid. You told me that Pamela and Rich argued in the morning before they went to Art in the Park, but you didn't tell me the real reason."

"Yes, I did. It was about Chip."

"It wasn't about Chip. It was about Rich's wanting to fire you, wasn't it?"

"No, no," she stopped and looked away.

"Mrs. Bramble?"

"How do you know that?"

"Pamela told me herself, but you never mentioned it."

"I. . . I didn't take it seriously," she stammered.

"Oh, but you did. Isn't that the reason you didn't tell me about it in the first place?"

"Oh, all right! Yes, Rich wanted to get rid of me. After ten years! To save money! That's crazy! Money's never been a problem around here."

"If money wasn't the reason, why do you think Rich wanted to fire you?"

"Jealousy I suppose. Pamela depends on me for everything. He didn't like it that she treats me like family."

"But, as you say, you've been here ten years. Why would he want to fire you *now*, if money wasn't an issue?"

Mrs. Bramble shrugged. "No idea, but I do know he'd brought it up before, more than once. Pamela always talked him out of it, and I'm pretty sure she would have done it again, but we'll never know."

"With Rich gone, your job must be secure; that is, unless Pamela ends up in prison."

"There is absolutely *no way* that sweet lady did anything to harm her husband, and I wouldn't do anything to hurt her, if you're implying that I stabbed Rich."

"No, I don't think you stabbed Rich," I said. What I didn't say, but was obvious, was that Mrs. Bramble certainly had a motive. On the other hand, she probably had an alibi, too; surely the police would have checked. I decided I'd already carried my inquiries far enough with her. I didn't want to make an enemy of Mrs. Bramble since Pamela relied on her so heavily. "I'd better get back to Pamela."

I started to turn, but Mrs. Bramble grabbed my arm to stop me.

"I heard you solved some other cases. You can help her, can't you? Please!"

"I'm going to try. Unfortunately, right now, we don't have much to go on. If you think of anything—anything at all—that could have a bearing on the case, please let me know." She nodded.

"Right now, the best thing you can do for her is to keep on doing what you're doing. Pamela needs some TLC. Take care of her."

"I always do."

When I returned to the den, I was surprised to see Pamela holding her cellphone.

"I just tried to call Fred, but he's not answering. I left a message for him to call me back."

"It's really important that we get a hold of him as soon as possible. Is there someone else from the office who might be able to track him down?"

"Maybe the sales manager. I can check with her. She won't be in the office today. I'll have to look up her cell number. It would be on Rich's phone, but the police must have it. Let me check Rich's desk in the study. He might have a list there."

Since Pamela hadn't asked me to help her search, I stayed put in the den until she returned.

"No luck."

"Who answers calls at the main office in Phoenix on the weekend?"

"Nobody. The phone system automatically prompts anybody calling to leave a message. I guess we'll just have to wait until Fred calls me back."

"Let's see if we can find out if the sales manager has a landline," I said, as I pulled out my phone. "What's her name?"

"Sheila Granville."

"I'll see what I can find." I began searching for Sheila's information, and I was somewhat amazed to find that there was a white pages listing for her. At least, I thought it was the same woman. How many Sheila Granvilles could there be in Phoenix?

"I think this is it," I told Pamela. I handed her my phone so that she could see the number.

"Here goes nothing," Pamela said as she punched the number in, and the phone started to ring.

Chapter 28

Again, there was no answer. I could hear the phone prompt to leave a message just as the doorbell rang, and Mrs. Bramble left the kitchen to see who it was.

"Oh, my! How beautiful!" we heard Mrs. Bramble exclaim. Saying that she'd try to call Sheila back later, Pamela set her phone down to go to the door herself. I trailed behind her and saw Mrs. Bramble directing a young man to set a huge floral arrangement on a side table just inside the door. Right behind him, a woman about my age held a potted plant in each hand. I looked past her and saw two white delivery vans, each from a different florist.

While Pamela signed for the deliveries, Mrs. Bramble took charge of the potted plants, setting them on either side of the floral arrangement and moving them around until their positions suited her.

As the delivery people departed, Pamela stepped forward to close the front door, but she stopped when a red Toyota Camry pulled up in front, and Chip jumped out. He jogged to the door and embraced Pamela while Mrs. Bramble watched with a look of disgust on her face before stalking off to the kitchen.

"Why don't you go back to the den," I suggested. "I'll get you some coffee, Chip. Pamela, would you like another cup?"

"No, thanks, Amanda."

Mrs. Bramble was pulling a bowl out from under the island counter and muttering to herself when I approached and asked her to please brew another pot of coffee.

"I take it you're not a big fan of Chip's," I ventured.

"I don't really dislike Chip; he's caused a lot of problems for Pamela around here, that's all. I don't think he should be hanging around now, *especially* now. It looks bad. Pamela's got enough to worry about without him butting in."

"I think he's just trying to offer her support. They're friends, after all, and they're bound to see each other at the gallery fairly often, now that—"

"Now that Rich is no longer in the picture you mean."

"Well, when you put it that way, I grant you it doesn't sound too good, but Chip's gone out of his way to avoid seeing Pamela ever since Rich wanted her to quit as gallery director so that she wouldn't be around him."

"But that's exactly my point. It's as though he can't wait to see her. He never should have given her that demo painting."

"Hmm, well, I guess what's done is done."

"Looks like the coffee's ready. Let me get the tray."

"No need. Chip's coffee can go in a mug," I said, pointing to a rack of mugs hanging near the cupboard. "I know he doesn't take milk or sugar, so just make his black."

With a scowl, Mrs. Bramble grabbed a mug and filled it with coffee.

"Thanks so much. One cup should do it. Pamela said she didn't want any more."

When I entered the den, Pamela and Chip, who were sitting next to each other on the sofa, stopped whispering. Chip jumped up and took the mug of coffee before moving to a chair.

"Thanks, Amanda."

"What did I miss?" I asked, not willing to ignore their confab.

"Oh, uh, nothing much. Chip was just filling me in on business at the gallery."

I looked at Pamela, and I could tell she was fibbing, which made me even more curious about their conversation, but I decided to drop it for now. I figured it would be easier to wheedle out what they'd been discussing later from Chip, rather than from Pamela.

Unwilling to leave Chip alone with her, I decided to hang around for a while, settling into a plush armchair next to Chip. Although I hadn't accomplished much in the way of my investigation, I'd learned that we definitely needed to talk to Fred Wagner, and I was frustrated that Pamela hadn't been able to get in touch with him. It seemed to me that the vice-president and controller of a company that had just suffered the loss of its owner should be more responsive to the new owner.

I was certain that Rich had left everything to Pamela. Most likely he'd left a will, but even if he didn't have one, under Arizona statutes, she stood to inherit all his assets since they had no children. It irritated me that Fred might be playing eighteen rounds on the golf course instead of attending to business, but, of course, I really had no idea what the man was doing.

Pamela and Chip had stopped conversing, and we sat in silence for a few minutes while Chip drank his coffee and Pamela spaced out. Suddenly, she jumped up, muttering that she should check the cards that had accompanied the flowers and plants that were now sitting on the side table in the foyer.

"Chip," I said in a low voice so that Pamela couldn't hear me, "what were you and Pamela really talking about when I came in?"

Before he could answer, we heard the slapping of Pamela's slingback sandals on the tile floor in the hallway.

He put his fingers to his lips. "Shhh, she'll hear us. We'll talk later."

Puzzled as to what the big secret was, I listened while Pamela read us the cards she'd received, one from Ralph, another from Dorothy, and a third from Susan. We all agreed that the flowers they'd sent were beautiful. I was afraid reading the condolences would send Pamela into another crying jag, but she managed not to shed any tears, although her hands were trembling as she held each card and read it to us.

When she finished, Chip stood and declared that he needed to get going so that he could get to work in time. "I don't want to leave Dad too shorthanded. One of our delivery drivers quit last night, so we're already one down, and Saturday's our busiest day."

I decided it was time for me to leave, too, and the three of us walked to the front door. I gave Pamela a quick hug, and she assured me she'd call as soon as she heard from Fred or Sheila.

"What was that all about, Chip?" I asked as soon as Pamela closed the door, "and why don't you want Pamela to know you're telling me about it?"

"Not now, Amanda," Chip begged. "I really do have to get to work."

"Chip!"

"'Bye, Amanda. See you later." With that, Chip hopped into his new red car and took off, kicking up a bit of dust in his wake. I coughed and waved my hand in front of my face before quickly ducking into my SUV and turning the air conditioning to high.

I had no intention of letting Chip avoid my question since there was a chance that whatever he and Pamela were discussing might have some bearing on her case. I'd have to wait until I could catch him when he wasn't at work or on the way, though.

Frustrated that I hadn't really learned anything that would help me find out who killed Rich, I drove home and spent most of the afternoon painting. As was my normal practice, I had three canvases in various stages of completion. This afternoon, my top priority would have to go to the portrait of a pair of German shepherds that was nearly complete. I'd done some work on it several days back, but the painting seemed to lack something.

Standing back and gazing at it, I was pleased with my depiction of the dogs and thought I'd captured their enthusiasm and vitality.

Finally, I decided the background needed some color correction with a few highlights. As I worked on the background, I felt satisfied that I was solving the issue that had been nagging me.

"I think that's got it," I said to myself when I finished and once more stood back to gaze at the portrait. "What do you think, Laddie?"

"Woof!"

"I'm glad you agree. Now how about a game of fetch since you've been such a good boy all afternoon?"

Laddie rushed to me as I set my paints aside, and I didn't have the heart to make him wait while I put them away and cleaned my brushes, so we headed to the backyard where he scooped up his hard rubber ball, ran around me in circles, and then, looking up at me expectantly, obligingly dropped it at my feet.

I tossed the ball, and he bolted after it, and then circled back to me. He let me take it from his mouth and watched as I tossed it again, this time a little bit farther away.

After playing fetch for several minutes, I noticed that Laddie was starting to slow down, so we retreated to the shade of the patio, where, panting, he settled happily beside me when I plunked myself in a lawn chair.

"Good boy," I said as I stroked his silky fur.

With nobody around, except my furry companions, I couldn't discuss any theories I came up with with anybody, but I realized I was pretty much fresh out of ideas. Briefly, I felt tempted to call Belle, but I restrained myself. After all, she was on vacation in Michigan, and I was sure she and Dennis would be involved in some activities with her children and grandchildren, especially on Saturday.

"I guess it's just you and me, Laddie," I murmured, "and Mona Lisa, of course."

I thought I heard a little whimper of protest at my mention of my calico kitty, but, then again, I could have imagined it.

Idly, I picked up my cellphone. It was getting close to time for Emma to come home from work, but she was planning on have dinner with Matt before they attended the new production that the Lonesome Valley Little Theater was debuting this evening, so I'd be dining alone.

A couple hours later, when Emma had come and gone and I'd had a not-so-delicious dinner of leftover spaghetti, I was expecting Brian to call to let me know how his meetings with the corporate bigwigs had gone, but when my phone rang, it wasn't Brian, but Pamela.

After waiting all day to hear from Fred or Sheila, she'd had some news, and it wasn't good.

Chapter 29

"Fred's in the hospital with a punctured lung and broken ribs. According to Sheila, he was hit by a truck Friday evening, but Fred's girlfriend was so shaken up that she didn't happen to think to let anybody in the company know until now. Sheila called me as soon as she heard the news."

"No wonder you couldn't get in touch with him," I said, feeling a little guilty that I'd imagined the man nonchalantly strolling around the golf course this morning when, in fact, he'd been an accident victim.

"That's not all," Pamela told me. "His girlfriend saw what happened, and she's sure it was no accident."

"Someone hit him deliberately?" I was trying to wrap my head around a vague idea that Fred had killed Rich, and someone else had tried to kill Fred. It didn't really make much sense, though, and I realized that the two events probably weren't connected at all. I was struggling with the motive angle and asking myself what Fred would have to gain by stabbing his boss. The only thing I could come up with might be that he wanted to be president of the company, but that didn't make sense, either, because there would be no guarantee that he'd become president. As the sole owner of a privately held company, Pamela could chose anyone she wanted.

"Amanda?"

I realized I'd drifted a bit when I heard Pamela say my name, and I also realized I'd missed something she'd been trying to tell me.

"Sorry, what was that again, Pamela?"

"Fred's girlfriend saw what happened just as she was leaving work. Fred was waiting for her, and he'd just stepped out of his car when a truck that had been parked in the lot started up and headed right toward him. She said it never slowed down."

"That's awful! The poor guy! She didn't happen to get the license plate, did she?"

"No; it all happened too fast. She told me she was on her cellphone calling 9-1-1 while the truck was speeding off. By the way, you'll never guess who Fred's girlfriend is."

"Do I know her?"

"Yes and no. She's one of the six o'clock anchors at Channel 11."

"Cheri Logan? Seriously? She's really high profile. I heard she might be tapped for a promotion to the network in New York."

"I wouldn't be surprised. I know she's popular."

"Do you think Fred would follow her to New York if she gets a new job there?"

"I don't know. I hadn't even thought about that. What would I do without Fred in charge? I know next to nothing about Rich's business."

As soon as the words were out of my mouth, I regretted saying them. Pamela had enough on her plate without worrying about taking care of Rich's business. Unfortunately, it would fall to her to arrange for new management if Fred didn't stay.

"Let's put that aside for a moment so we can concentrate on getting the charges against you dropped. Maybe Fred can give us some insight into what was going on at the company before Rich's death. We definitely need to speak with him."

"I know. I suggested a meeting to Cheri, but she said Fred needed some time to recover. The doctors indicated that he'd be in the hospital for several days, at least. She did say she'd call me with an update tomorrow, though."

"Well, all right. I don't suppose we can rush it; let's hope Fred will be up to talking in a few days."

"I don't have a clue what to do about the company," Pamela wailed. "Rich seldom talked about his business with me, and, to be frank, I didn't pay as much attention as I should have when he did."

"Pamela, don't beat yourself up over it. I doubt that you'll have to make any decisions immediately. I'm sure one of the other managers can take charge until Fred's ready to come back to work. Maybe the arrangements have already been made. Why don't you check with Sheila tomorrow?"

"OK; I'll do that. Everything's so overwhelming!"

I wished I'd been able to allay some of Pamela's concerns, but the truth was that I felt worried about them, too. I hoped that there wouldn't be some huge, unpleasant surprise that Fred would reveal about R. J. Smith Software, but I also knew that I needed to keep my eye on the ball. If the homicide charge against Pamela wasn't dropped, Rich's software company would be the least of her worries.

Thinking that Brian would probably call me, I stayed up late, but never heard from him. I figured he might have had to go out to dinner with the people from corporate headquarters, and I didn't want to bother him if that was the case, so I decided I shouldn't call him.

Hoping no news was good news, I roused Laddie from his evening nap, and he followed me into the bedroom, jumped up on the bed, and was fast asleep before I finished brushing my teeth.

I wasn't long behind him, and I slept soundly until, eager for his morning walk, he woke me at five o'clock. I could have easily slept another hour or two, but as a dutiful pet parent, I rolled out of bed, hurriedly dressed, and snapped Laddie's leash onto his collar.

We went out the back door, so we wouldn't disturb Emma. I'd heard her come in just before I'd climbed into bed, and I knew she'd be sound asleep at this hour.

Laddie and I headed to our usual destination—the little city park a few blocks from home. Although the park wasn't too busy, we saw a few regular dog walkers and their canine companions.

Laddie seemed even perkier than usual, so I decided that, instead of going straight home, we'd take a circuitous route, winding our way along the outskirts of our neighborhood and returning from a different direction than usual.

By this time, I was looking forward to a cup of coffee. I opened the back door, took off Laddie's leash, and headed straight to the kitchen to make the brew. With Mona Lisa curled up beside her, Emma was still sleeping peacefully. I tiptoed around the kitchen, trying my best to be as quiet as possible, but I accidentally clinked my mug against the tile countertop. Emma rolled over but didn't awaken, and Mona Lisa didn't stir.

With Laddie at my side, I took my coffee, went into the studio, and quietly closed the door.

Sipping the hot beverage, I checked my email on my laptop while Laddie sat next to me, his head resting on my lap. Although I found plenty of advertising, there weren't any messages that required a response, so I closed my laptop and petted my affection-seeking retriever with my left hand while using my right to handle my coffee cup.

"Time to get to work," I announced after a few minutes. Laddie knew what that meant, and he trotted to his bed and flopped down when I stood up.

Since I'd completed the pet portrait of the engaging German shepherds, there were now two canvasses to finish: a dreamy landscape painted in the expressionistic abstract style I favored and the more realistic pet portrait of Jennifer's beagle Betsy. I hadn't worked on the landscape for several days, so I decided to devote at least an hour to it before returning to Betsy's portrait.

It turned out to be closer to two hours until I heard the creak of the hide-a-bed, and I knew my daughter was up. The noise was loud enough that it woke Laddie from his nap. He ran to the closed door and waited for me to open it. As soon as I did, he rushed to his bowl in the kitchen and looked at me with anticipation. Meowing, Mona Lisa wandered into the kitchen, her tail held high.

"OK; I get the hint." I rinsed their bowls, filled them, and set them back down at opposite ends of the kitchen. I could hear the shower running, but I couldn't remember whether Emma had to work or not. Since the thought of a leisurely breakfast that I didn't have to prepare myself sounded good, I thought that Emma and I could go out for breakfast, if she wasn't due at the feed store. Of course, all the restaurants would be busy on a Sunday, but I didn't feel so hungry that I couldn't stand to wait for a while to be seated.

When Emma emerged from the bathroom dressed in shorts and a gauzy turquoise blue summer top, I knew she wasn't going to work.

"How about some coffee, Emma?"

"Sounds good."

I filled a mug three quarters full and then topped it off with milk. Although the combination didn't appeal to me, my daughter liked to have lots of milk in her coffee.

"Thanks, Mom," she said, as I handed her the mug. "Do you feel like going out to breakfast?"

"I was just about to suggest that myself. Where would you like to go?"

"Maybe we could try that new pastry place downtown. A couple of people from work went there last week, and they were raving about the crêpes."

"All right. Let's try it." Although I really liked crêpes, I hadn't had any for quite a while. Since making them wasn't in my cooking repertoire, I certainly wouldn't be having any at home. "Give me a few minutes to change, and we'll be on our way."

Laddie followed me to the bedroom where he watched me exchange my paint-splattered t-shirt for a pink cotton blouse and my sneakers for sandals. Of course, he recognized the signals that I was about to depart, and he gave me a please-don't-leave-me-Mommy look when Emma and I went out the door.

"Be a good boy, Laddie," I told him, gently easing the door closed behind us. If we'd been going to a restaurant with a dog-friendly patio, I would have taken him along with us, but I knew the restaurant

Emma had chosen had only inside seating because it had taken over the same downtown space where a small cafe had previously operated.

I found a parking spot on Main Street near our destination. We noticed several groups of people milling around outside. A few of them sat on benches provided by Lonesome Valley's Downtown Merchants' Association, while others stood casually chatting as they waited to be seated.

"I'll go get us on the waiting list," Emma volunteered.

She came back in a few minutes holding a buzzer that would alert us when our turn for a table came.

"They said it's going to be about twenty minutes," she said.

"Really? That's not bad at all. I thought it would be longer with all these people waiting."

As I heard a familiar voice behind me, I turned around, but I never would have recognized the man standing there if his wife hadn't been right beside him.

"Hi, stranger," he said. "We haven't seen you for a while."

Chapter 30

"Jerry?"

"In the flesh."

It had been quite a while since I'd seen Jerry Madison, my veterinarian, and his wife. Several months ago, I'd painted a portrait of their dogs for them in exchange for veterinary care for Laddie and Mona Lisa.

Jerry, who'd previously been clean shaven with short hair, now sported a beard and long hair. No wonder I'd barely recognized him.

Katie, Jerry's wife, giggled at my look of astonishment. "He's getting ready to participate in a mountain man reenactment this fall," she explained. "I can't wait until it's over, and he can shave again. That beard is just too much for me."

"Hey," Jerry protested, rubbing his hand over his scraggly gray beard. "I need to look the part."

"I think you're succeeding," I said, and we all laughed.

After I introduced Emma, we all moved into a spot in the shade to wait for our tables.

"I can't believe Rich Smith's wife was charged with his murder," Katie said. "You must know her from the Roadrunner, don't you?"

"Yes, she's a friend of mine. I'm sure she didn't do it. I'm hoping the district attorney will drop the charges. I didn't realize you knew Pamela and Rich."

"I don't know Pamela too well," Katie admitted, "although I've met her a few times, but Jerry played golf with Rich and a couple of other guys fairly often."

"He seemed like an okay guy," Jerry said. "A little jealous, though, now that I think about it. He used to call his wife while we were out on the golf course, almost like he was checking up on her."

"We noticed the same thing—at the Roadrunner, I mean."

"Maybe she'd had enough of it," Katie speculated.

"Despite his jealousy, Pamela loved Rich," I assured Katie. "She'd never have done anything to hurt him."

"Maybe it had something to do with his business," Jerry said.

"Why do you think so?" His comment had me on the alert since I'd been thinking along those same lines.

"Something he said the last time we played golf. I guess it was maybe about three weeks ago now. Rich mentioned that he'd had an offer to buy his business."

"He was considering selling?"

"Yes, he was mulling it over, but then he said he was also thinking about taking the business in a different direction."

"I wonder what he meant by that."

"No idea. To tell you the truth, I was having a bad day on the links and I was more concerned about setting up my next shot than I was about what Rich was saying."

"He didn't mention any specifics, then?"

"I don't think so. Not that I recall, anyway."

We were interrupted when the buzzer that Emma was holding started to make noise.

"Looks like our table's ready," I said. "It was nice to see you."

"By the way, I meant to tell you how much we're enjoying your painting of our pups," Katie said.

"Thank you. That's good to hear." I smiled. "It's always nice to have a satisfied customer."

"Don't forget you're our customer, too," Jerry reminded me. "I haven't seen Laddie or Mona Lisa at the clinic lately."

"Laddie and Mona Lisa have both been just fine, but Mona Lisa's check-up is coming up in a couple weeks if I remember right."

"We'll see you then. Nice to meet you, Emma."

"You, too," Emma murmured, nudging me lightly. "Mom, we'd better get going or they might give our table to someone else."

I flashed Katie and Jerry a smile before following Emma through the crowd and into the bustling restaurant where we were quickly seated and given menus.

"Wow! I've never seen so many different kinds of crêpes on one menu. It's going to be hard to decide what to order."

"I think I'll go with one savory and one sweet," Emma said.

"Sounds like a good idea."

We finished scanning our menus and settled on our choices just as our server showed up to take our orders and pour our coffee.

After the server hustled off with our orders, Emma told me she thought that her father was beginning to accept her decision to attend NAU in the fall. Remembering the quarrel the two had a few days earlier, I was surprised to hear that Ned might be changing his mind.

"I called him back yesterday evening," Emma said. "It was after Matt dropped me off, and you were already in bed, but I knew Dad would still be up."

"He always was a night owl," I agreed, remembering that my former husband often hadn't come to bed until the wee hours of the morning. I never could understand how he managed to function on so little sleep.

"Yeah, well, even if he'd been sleeping, the baby's screaming would have put an end to that. I've never heard a kid yell so loudly. Candy made Dad take him while she went back to bed."

"How were you able to talk when he was taking care of the baby?"

"I guess he's got some hands-free baby carrier, kind of like a sling, and he put him in there and walked around with him while we were talking."

"Umm; that's good," I said. I was trying to imagine Ned comforting a crying baby, but I was having a hard time conjuring up the image. He'd barely interacted with Dustin and Emma until they were grade-school age. As for getting up in the middle of the night with a bawling child or changing a diaper, forget about it: that had never happened. Still, I was glad that he seemed to be taking an interest in his newest offspring far earlier than he had with our children.

"Anyway, he backed off. He's still not too happy about my transferring to NAU, but he's quit fighting me about it. He wants me to come visit before the semester starts. I guess maybe I'll go for a few days, but I'm not really looking forward to seeing Candy."

"Maybe you and your dad can spend some time together, just the two of you."

"I hope so. I mean the little guy's cute and all, and I don't mind taking care of him once in a while, but Candy thinks of me only as a babysitter, and she usually arranges for her and Dad to go out somewhere whenever I'm in town. I told him that, too, and he promised this time will be different. I guess we'll see."

Emma's sigh told me that she wasn't exactly sure about that, but she seemed to be inching towards a grudging acceptance of the huge change in our family life that our divorce and Ned's new marriage had brought about.

Evidently, Emma had said all she wanted to say about her father because she changed the subject and began telling me about the classes she and Matt would be taking at NAU in the fall. Although they weren't enrolled in the same courses, they'd carefully arranged their schedules so that they would have to be on campus only two days a week and they could drive to Flagstaff together. They knew Dennis would accommodate them, and they'd be free to work the other days in the feed store.

The crowd had begun to thin at the restaurant, and since people weren't waiting for tables any longer, we enjoyed a leisurely brunch before heading home to an enthusiastic greeting from Laddie and a more restrained one from Mona Lisa, who rubbed herself against Emma's ankles but then scampered away and hid behind the sofa.

I admit I was feeling a bit lazy, and I considered skipping studio time. I puttered around for a few minutes before deciding that I really should get to work. Still, I procrastinated for another hour before finally forcing myself to pick up my brush and continue working on the landscape that was beginning to shape up the way I'd envisioned it. As soon as I began painting, I forgot my earlier reluctance and had no problem focusing on my artwork. Despite being very close to completing the pet portrait Jennifer had commissioned, I'd chosen to work on the landscape, instead of Betsy's picture. I was well aware my choice was another instance of my bad habit of procrastination, but I rationalized my decision, telling myself that I could complete Betsy's portrait the next day.

It wasn't until Pamela called later that afternoon that I realized I wouldn't have nearly as much time to work on the portrait as I'd thought.

I'd just stopped painting long enough to take a short break and have some limeade when Pamela called me to let me know that Cheri Logan, Fred's girlfriend, had called to report that Fred wanted to talk to Pamela, but he wasn't up to it yet. He'd suggested that maybe Pamela could come to the hospital to see him on Tuesday morning, and she'd agreed that she'd be there at ten.

"You'll come with me, won't you, Amanda? I really need back-up."

"Yes. I'm scheduled to work at the Roadrunner that morning, but I'm sure I can find somebody who's willing to switch days with me."

"All right. Good. Pick you up at eight?"

"Are you sure you want to drive, Pamela? I don't mind."

"It's fine. Driving gives me something to concentrate on, and I don't worry so much."

"OK. I hope we'll be able to find out something that'll help. Anyway, you definitely need to find out what's going on at the company."

"I know. I told Nate, and he agrees. I asked him if he wanted to come with us, but he said he has too many jobs lined up. I didn't push it because I know he lost some business because of having to deal with my problems."

I assured Pamela I'd be ready to go on Tuesday and immediately opened my laptop to check on the Roadrunner's schedule. When I scanned through the upcoming week, I noticed that Chip would be attending the gallery Monday morning, along with Valerie, who taught art at the high school. Since Valerie was off work for the summer, I figured her schedule might be flexible. If she'd agree to switch Monday morning for my scheduled shift Tuesday morning, I could not only accommodate Pamela so that we could visit Fred in the hospital Tuesday, but I could also try to find out what Chip was avoiding telling me.

Keeping my fingers crossed, I phoned Valerie and asked her whether she'd mind swapping Monday morning for Tuesday morning.

"I have an appointment in Phoenix Tuesday morning," I explained.

"It wouldn't have anything to do with Pamela, would it?" Valerie asked.

"As a matter of fact, it would, but I can't really get into the particulars right now."

Obviously, it was no secret that I was trying to exonerate Pamela.

"Well, I wish you luck. I still can't believe Pamela was arrested. Of course, I'd be happy to trade places with you."

"Thanks, Valerie, I appreciate the favor."

"No problem. I'm free as a bird until school starts, so it doesn't really make much difference to me what days I work at the Roadrunner."

Although there were plenty of other people I could have asked to trade places, I was pleased that Valerie had made it easy on the first try.

Tomorrow morning, I intended to find out exactly what Chip had been holding back.

Chapter 31

Emma poked her head into the studio.

"Mom, would you like me to fix us a salad for dinner?"

"Oh, sure, Emma. That would be nice. I thought you'd be going out with Matt."

"Not tonight. He promised to help his grandparents with some painting."

"That's nice of him after he worked all day."

"What can I say? He's a nice guy! Dinner in fifteen minutes."

Figuring that I'd be able to have a couple of hours to work on Betsy's portrait after dinner before I lost the light, I put away the oils I'd been using for my landscape and set up my palette for the pet portrait so that everything would be ready as soon as we finished dinner.

I hadn't heard from Brian since his call Friday telling me he wouldn't be home for the weekend. I wondered if the corporate bigwigs could still be in town and whether he was having to entertain them as well as suffer their intense scrutiny. He certainly hadn't seemed happy that they'd sprung an unexpected visit—or was it an inspection?—on him. I toyed with the idea of calling or texting him, but, like the previous day, I was afraid that an interruption might be bothersome, so I resolved to wait until he called me.

His call didn't come until much later. I'd already decided to go to bed when my cellphone rang.

"Hi, stranger!" I said brightly, but my cheery tone didn't match his.

"Sorry I wasn't able to call sooner," he replied glumly.

"You sound tired. Bad weekend?"

"More like no weekend, and I'm exhausted. These corporate guys aren't exactly fun to be around. They kept grilling me about every little detail of the operation. I barely had a chance to breathe. They just left for the airport to take the red eye back to Dallas, but they mentioned that they might be back later in the month. I hope my job's not in jeopardy, but I couldn't really get a good read on them."

"Oh, Brian. I'm so sorry you had to put up with them and on your days off, too."

"Well, technically, according to them, I guess I *have* no days off. They definitely expect me to be available 24/7. When I happened to mention that I usually spend weekends at home in Lonesome Valley, it went over like a lead balloon."

"What are you going to do?"

"Not much I *can* do, but I might have to stay here more on the weekends."

"Oh, Brian."

"I know. I'm not crazy about the idea, either. When I worked on the rig, I got used to having time off when I really *was* off. I get that they think the manager should be available in case of an emergency, but I don't see that staying down here every weekend is absolutely necessary. I suppose we'll just have to wait and see what happens," he said with a sigh.

The rest of our brief conversation didn't lighten Brian's mood. Resisting my impulse to tell him not to worry, I urged him to get some sleep. In the months since I'd met him, Brian had never mentioned any problems at work, and until now, I'd thought his new job had been going quite well, so I was shocked to learn that he thought he might lose it.

Knowing that there wasn't anything I could do to help him didn't make me feel any better. As I lay in bed later, racking my brain for a way to make him feel better, I thought that perhaps I could spend some weekends in Southern Arizona, when he couldn't come home to Lonesome Valley, but I wouldn't be able to get an early start by leaving on Friday afternoon to travel, as was Brian's routine, because I was locked into Friday evening studio tours. Even though I often didn't sell a painting during the tours, they served as a great introduction to my art. People sometimes came back, even weeks later, to make a purchase or commission a pet portrait, and I frequently sold my hand-dyed abstract silk scarves on Friday nights, too.

Perhaps, things would settle down for Brian at work, and we wouldn't have to alter our routine at all. I tried to focus on that optimistic thought as I drifted off to sleep.

In the morning, I worried about Brian's plight as I went through my usual routine, but I had to switch focus when I arrived at the gallery a few minutes before my scheduled shift at nine. The lights were already on, and the front door unlocked, so Chip had already arrived. I was determined to pin him down because I was sure he was holding back some information, and I was beginning to think that whatever he knew might not be favorable to Pamela. Otherwise, I doubted that he'd hesitate to let me in on the secret he was keeping.

I stepped inside, but Chip wasn't in the gallery, so he'd probably gone upstairs to his studio for a minute. Knowing that he might not be happy when he found out I'd switched shifts with Valerie, I braced myself for a verbal tussle with him the moment I tried to pry his information from him. In the meantime, I set about doing some light dusting while I waited for him to appear.

He never showed up, though.

Instead, Susan surprised me when she came out of the office with the cash and change to set up the register for the day. Susan was as surprised to see me as I was at finding that she was working this morning, rather than Chip.

"Hi, Amanda. I thought Valerie was on the schedule today."

"She was. I traded places with her because I'm going to Phoenix tomorrow with Pamela so that we can talk to the vice-president of Rich's company."

"You think maybe he could be involved in Rich's murder?"

"I wondered at first, but now that he's been the victim of a hit-and-run himself, I'm thinking maybe the person who ran him down might have something to do with it because Fred's girlfriend thought the driver who hit him did it deliberately. So maybe Fred knows something that could help us. I admit I may be grasping at straws, but it seems to me that there's a huge question mark about Rich's finances."

"Right. Putting a mortgage on the house without Pamela knowing speaks volumes."

"Yes, and wanting to get rid of the housekeeper that they've had for ten years. I find that very odd."

"So do I. I know how much Pamela depends on Mrs. Bramble. She'd never want to fire her."

"If the financial angle doesn't pan out, we're back to square one again."

"That's not good. Poor Pamela! Every time I talk to her, she breaks down and starts to cry. Under the circumstances, it's no wonder she's distraught. Do you think she'll be able to handle the trip?"

"I hope so. She insisted on driving. She told me concentrating on the road helps take her mind off other things. By the way, I thought Chip was supposed to be here this morning. Did he ask you to change places with him?"

"No. I asked him. I realized that I'd scheduled a dentist's appointment on my Roadrunner day."

Evidently, Chip's switcheroo had nothing to do with mine. I thought maybe he'd learned I was going to take Valerie's place, so he had Susan take his. Instead, it was purely coincidental. I told myself to get a grip.

Since the Roadrunner wasn't busy, Susan and I spent our shift going over everything we knew or thought we knew about Rich's death, but, try as we might, we weren't able to further our investigation at all. If I learned nothing of significance from Fred tomorrow, I didn't know what I was going to do.

Chapter 32

Our quiet half-day at the Roadrunner ended when Dawn and Dorothy came in at one to take over for the afternoon.

"It feels kind of weird being here without Pamela," Dawn commented. "Dave let slip that Bill Belmont doesn't think they should have arrested Pamela, but the chief pressured them into it." She quickly added, "Please don't tell Dave I said anything!"

"I won't, but Lieutenant Belmont actually admitted to me that he was getting some pressure from the chief, so I'm not surprised to hear it. Of course, I haven't talked to the lieutenant lately. I'm not exactly in his good graces after what happened with Nate."

"Dave has his doubts about Pamela's arrest, too, but there's nothing he can do. The case is in the district attorney's hands now."

"Let's hope some new evidence comes to light," Susan said, "so that the real killer can be arrested."

"Amen to that," Dorothy agreed.

Susan and I left the gallery and parted ways out front since we had parked in opposite directions, but, before we said good-bye, I promised to let Susan know if the trip to Phoenix produced any leads in our investigation.

On the way home, I swung by the supermarket to pick up some fresh fruit and vegetables. I didn't have a lot of storage space in my small refrigerator, so I usually made a couple trips to the grocery store each week. Early Monday afternoon was a good time to go because the store wouldn't be very busy, and I usually could get in and out in a few minutes.

I was checking an avocado for ripeness when I heard a familiar voice behind me. I turned to see Mrs. Bramble picking up a bag of lemons. She noticed me at the same time, gave a little wave, and came my way.

"I hear you're going to Phoenix with Pamela tomorrow," she said without preamble. "I really wish she wouldn't drive. I told her I didn't think it was a good idea in her state, but she insisted."

"I know. I did offer to drive. If it becomes too much for her, I still can."

"You're a good friend to her, but, as you know, she can be stubborn at times." Mrs. Bramble's eyes filled with tears. "I'm so worried about her."

I gently squeezed her arm. "We all are."

"I'm so afraid she's going to end up in prison for a crime she didn't commit."

"I'll do my very best to help her."

"I know you're trying, but you can't promise she'll go free, can you?"

"Unfortunately, no, but I am hoping to find some new evidence."

"I'm sorry," she said, pulling a tissue from her purse and blotting her eyes. "It's not your fault she was arrested. I'm still suspicious of that brother of hers."

"But the police let him go because he has an alibi for the time of the murder."

"Uh, huh. I don't know about that. The cops better have checked and double-checked any alibi he claims he has. He's a slippery one."

I was about to ask Mrs. Bramble why she thought Nate was "a slippery one," as she put it, but we were joined by a familiar-looking tall man before I had the chance.

"Amanda, this is my husband John," she said. "John, Amanda Trent, Pamela's friend."

"Nice to meet you. Aren't you the lady who's trying to figure out who killed Smith?"

"I'm hoping to discover some new evidence to clear Pamela, yes."

"Well, more power to you. If you ask me, Pamela's better off without him."

Mrs. Bramble poked her husband.

"John, don't say such things. I know you didn't care much for the man, but don't ever let Pamela hear you say something like that."

"Sorry, dear," he mumbled, although I had the impression that he wasn't sorry at all.

"We'd better move along, so we can finish before the kids get out of their tennis lessons."

"We could have done our monthly shopping tomorrow, seeing as how Pamela gave you the day off."

"Well, she gave me this afternoon off, too, and I intend to take advantage of it. Then, I can cross at least one chore off my to-do list."

Still bickering, the two left the fruits and vegetables section of the store while I consulted my grocery list and finished my shopping.

As I made my way to the front of the supermarket to check out, I saw the couple halfway down the aisle where the drinks were displayed. John Bramble was putting a case of canned soda in their cart. I watched in disbelief as he grabbed another and set it on top of the first one, then picked up a couple cases of bottled water and put them into their shopping cart.

For a man who'd had back surgery, he didn't hesitate to lift what must have been over a hundred pounds of weight total, although not all at once. Even so, I'd assumed he was somewhat incapacitated because I remembered all the complaints he'd made about his health on social media. In fact, I'd pictured him as practically an invalid, but clearly that wasn't the case. Watching him and the way he moved, I'd never have suspected that he had any health problems at all. Yet, his wife solely supported their family, and they depended on health insurance from her job. The whole scenario seemed wrong, but perhaps I was missing something. I speculated that maybe John Bramble had good days and bad days. Today could have been one of the good ones.

Whatever the explanation, I intended to ask Pamela what she knew about Mrs. Bramble's husband. Although I certainly didn't plan to repeat what he said about her being better off without Rich, I was going to ask her if there'd ever been any bad blood between Rich and her housekeeper's husband, who just happened to bear more then a passing resemblance to her next-door neighbor Hal. Could John Bramble have been the man Emma saw talking to Rich the day he was stabbed at Art in the Park?

I couldn't wait to show Emma pictures he'd posted of himself on social media and find out whether she recognized him. If so, the case could be turning in a whole different direction.

Chapter 33

When I arrived home, Laddie was waiting at the kitchen door for me. I set my bags of groceries on the counter and stooped to give him a hug. He bounced around in excitement before heading for the back door. I let him out, stepped onto the patio, and watched him run around the yard. If Belle and Dennis hadn't been on vacation in Michigan, he would have enjoyed spending the morning with his little buddy Mr. Big.

He wasn't the only one who missed our next-door neighbors who wouldn't be coming home until next week. I'd picked up their mail and set it on their coffee table every day since they'd left. Our postal carrier usually didn't make it to our street until mid-afternoon, so it was too early to check for it now.

I called Laddie, and we went back in so that I could put the fruit and vegetables into the refrigerator. Mona Lisa, who hadn't budged from her perch atop her kitty tree, looked down at us with disdain, turned around, and curled up with her back to us.

"Not in a friendly mood, Mona Lisa?"

Of course, she didn't answer, but Laddie, who'd had enough of being alone with her all morning, stuck to my side while I sliced a pear and made myself a cheese sandwich. I slipped a couple of chunks of the

KILLER ART IN THE PARK

fruit into Laddie's bowl, and he quickly woofed them down before I had a chance to set my plate on the table.

He lay with his chin on my feet while I had my lunch, and when I got up, he stayed right with me when I went into the studio and got out my paints. Realizing that he probably wasn't going to settle down until I gave him some more attention, I set my palette down and petted him. Finally, after a few minutes, he calmed down and plopped onto his bed.

By the time I made my first brushstroke, he'd fallen asleep. I really envied his ability to go from being wide awake to sound asleep almost instantly. I'd lain awake many a night, not able to relax enough for sleep to come because I had something on my mind.

It took me about an hour and a half to paint the final details of Betsy's portrait, and Laddie slept the entire time. When I stood back to look at it from more of a distance, I knew I was done. It looked just as I had imagined it when I began to paint, and I thought Jennifer would be pleased to receive the painting earlier than promised, too. With a little flourish, I signed the portrait in the right lower corner and pronounced it complete.

Laddie woke with a start and barked a couple of times, but I wasn't the one who'd awakened him. He'd heard the rattle of our mailbox as the carrier opened it to deposit our mail, which undoubtedly would consist of a bunch of advertisements that would be going straight to the trash can and perhaps a bill or two.

When I checked the mail, there were no bills, only ads, so I discarded them before snapping Laddie's leash onto his collar, grabbing the key Belle had left me, and walking next door. Even though Laddie hadn't seen Mr. Big for several days, he looked around as though he were expecting to see him.

"Your pal will be back next week," I assured him as he sniffed the door as I struggled to turn the key while holding a stack of mail, including a thick magazine as well as the usual ads. There was already quite an accumulation of letters and circulars on the coffee table. I added to the pile, took a quick glance around to make sure everything was in order, locked the door on the way out, and walked Laddie back home across the side yard.

I had just one more task to do before I'd completed my business for the day. I grabbed my phone and laptop and took them to the patio. After playing fetch with Laddie, I settled in a lawn chair while he wandered around the backyard.

Before doing some research on John Bramble, I wanted to let Jennifer know that I'd completed Betsy's portrait.

"Fantastic!" she replied when I gave her the news. "I'd like to see it, but I guess it'll have to wait. I'm leaving this afternoon to spend a few days visiting my sister and her family."

"No problem. The paint needs to dry more, anyway. I was going to ask you if you'd like to come by the studio to see it although I'd suggest waiting at least a week before moving it to your house."

"All right. I hadn't really thought about it before, but I've heard that oil paint can take forever to dry."

"It can take a while, for sure, but I've found that it's not as much of a problem here as it was when I lived in Kansas City. Why don't you give me a call when you get back home, and we'll set up a time when you can come over to the studio."

"I will. I can't wait to see my baby captured on canvas!"

"Have a good trip, and I'll see you sometime after you get back."

After I finished my conversation with Jennifer, I put the phone down and picked up my laptop. My goal was to find some pictures of John Bramble that I could show to Emma. I didn't know why I hadn't noticed the similarity in looks between him and Hal before, when I'd first looked at their social media accounts. Although I'd searched several platforms, I'd found him on only one when I'd searched previously. After I tried again and came up with the same results, I realized that I hadn't delved too deeply into his account's history. I'd looked at his photos on his home page, but that was all.

I could understand now why I hadn't made the connection between Hal's appearance and John's. In his home page pictures, he was sitting down with his head either turned to the side or looking down. Although the pictures weren't very clear, he didn't look like a well man.

This time I set out to view all his photos in hopes of finding one that reminded me of the way he'd looked when I'd seen him in person for the first time. I soon discovered that most of his other pictures were of local scenery, but eventually I found one shot of him that I could show Emma. In it, he looked very much as he had today at the grocery store, not like the sick man shown in his home page pictures.

I texted Emma to ask her whether she needed me to pick her up from work at five, but she replied that, although Matt couldn't give her a ride because he was working late, one of her co-workers had volunteered to drop her off at home.

While I waited for her arrival, I chopped some apples and celery for a salad and tidied up the kitchen. As soon as Emma came in the front door and recovered from an effusive greeting from both Mona Lisa and Laddie, I pointed her to my laptop, which was sitting open on our tiny table and asked her to take a look and let me know what she thought. I didn't want to influence her in any way, so I didn't tell her what I was asking her to look at.

Emma tapped the keyboard, bringing the screen back to life and stared at John Bramble's picture. "Is this a picture of Hal Quinlan?" she asked. "It kind of looks like him, but not quite."

"Exactly what I thought, too, but, no, it's someone else. I wondered if he could be the man you saw talking to Rich at Art in the Park."

"Hmm. I suppose so, but I can't really say for certain. Who is he?"

"He's the husband of Pamela's housekeeper. His name's John Bramble."

"Oh, so he could be a suspect."

"That's what I'm thinking, but nothing's really clear at this point."

"I'm sorry I can't really identify either him or Hal. I just don't know for sure."

"Emma, that's all right. It was a long shot at best, but it's worth looking into him more, I think. Maybe Pamela can help fill in the blanks tomorrow. After all, Mrs. Bramble's worked for her for at least ten years, so I think she must know something about her husband."

"Promise me you'll be careful, Mom. I was totally freaked out when the plumber was arrested right here at the house. What if he had been the real killer? You could have been hurt."

"I promise. I don't want to worry you, Emma, but I think the most dangerous thing about our trip to Phoenix tomorrow will be fighting the traffic. Pamela and I are going to be visiting one of Rich's employees who's in the hospital. That seems pretty safe to me."

"Well, I suppose so. I just wouldn't want anything bad to happen to you. I feel like I've already lost Dad in a way," Emma said as she teared up.

Feeling awful that our divorce had caused Emma so much pain, I hugged her and gently pressed a tissue into her hand. "I'm so sorry, Emma."

"I know it wasn't your fault. Dad's the one to blame. I don't know if I can ever forgive him for what he did."

"We have to move on as best we can. There's no way to go back and change the past, and he is still your father, no matter what."

"I know. I love him, but I hate what he did."

I understood exactly how my daughter felt. Those were the same feelings I had myself right after Ned announced that he was going to divorce me and marry a woman not too much older than Emma. Eventually, though, I fell out of love with my husband and decided to make a new life for myself, one that didn't include Ned.

It wasn't the same for my daughter, though. Ned wouldn't always be my husband, but he would always be Emma's father, and I was hoping that she could reconcile with him as Dustin, who'd been furious with Ned when he'd first heard the news, had been able to do. It was taking Emma longer, quite a bit longer, in fact, but perhaps she'd eventually get there.

"Give it some time," I advised, knowing how trite I sounded, but Emma nodded in agreement.

Laddie and Mona Lisa had both rushed to her when she'd started to cry. She looked down at Mona Lisa crouched on her lap and Laddie pressed against her leg, petting Laddie with her left hand while she stroked Mona Lisa's soft fur with her right. "Sorry, guys; don't be upset," she murmured. "I'm OK now."

"Dinner in about half an hour?"

"Sure. Can I help?"

"You just take care of your little buddies there, and I'll take care of the food."

While I worked in the kitchen, I listened to Emma singing softly to Mona Lisa and Laddie, who both gazed at her with rapt attention. They all looked so cute I couldn't resist taking their picture with my cellphone during the serenade. Knowing I couldn't solve Emma's problem or do anything to make her feel better about our new family dynamics broke my heart. I hated seeing my daughter in pain. As much as I avoided thinking about my ex-husband, I couldn't help the anger I was feeling toward him right now for what he'd put Emma through.

Although Emma was quieter than usual during dinner, she perked up when Matt called her and suggested they go to a movie after he got off work at eight. She changed her clothes three or four times, and she'd finally settled on her outfit seconds before Matt showed up to whisk her away to the movie.

I'd barely had time to say "hello" and "good-bye" because the show started in a few minutes, and they wanted to be on their way.

After they left, I checked my cellphone to see whether I'd inadvertently turned the sound down because Brian hadn't yet called, and he normally would have by now. I was worried about him because he had sounded so down when we talked the day before, so I decided I'd give him a call, rather than waiting.

The phone rang several times, and I figured I'd be directed to voicemail, but, instead, I was surprised to hear a woman crisply pronounce

"Brian Hudson's phone." In fact, I was so taken aback that I was momentarily speechless.

"Hello?"

"Uh, may I speak to Brian please?"

"He's just stepped out for a moment. May I take a message?"

"Sure," I said. "Just tell him Amanda called."

"Last name?"

"Just tell him Amanda," I repeated before ending the call.

Now that I thought about it, I realized Brian must still be at work. He'd never mentioned that he had an assistant, but, of course, the manager of a large facility would have.

About ten minutes later, he called me back. "You rang?"

I was relieved that he sounded much happier than the last time we spoke.

"Yes. I was surprised you didn't answer your phone."

"Sorry about that. I left it with Kelli when I went out to check for damage. We just had a windstorm here, but, thankfully, I didn't find any problems. I was afraid one of the corporate bigwigs might call, and I didn't want to deal with that and storm damage at the same time."

"Well, I'm glad it didn't do any damage."

"So am I. I'm under the gun already. I don't need any more grief from some suit at corporate headquarters."

"You sound as though you're feeling better than you were yesterday."

"I am, and I apologize for my complaining. I may have overreacted, but I'm not used to being micromanaged."

"So do you think you need to stay there this weekend, or will you be coming home?"

"I'm planning on being in Lonesome Valley all weekend, but I'll probably drive up early Saturday morning since you have your studio tour Friday night anyway. We can go out for brunch and then maybe take Laddie for a hike in the old state park up in mountains in the afternoon. How's that sound?"

"That sounds good."

"All right. We'll plan on it then. What's going on with Pamela's case? I should have asked you about it yesterday."

As I filled Brian in on everything that had happened and the trip Pamela and I would be taking to Phoenix the next day, I felt happy that Brian sounded almost like his old self. He'd mentioned that perhaps he had overreacted, so I assumed he no longer thought his job was in jeopardy, but I could tell that he wasn't happy about the way the head office people were treating him.

I hoped he wouldn't suddenly quit on the spot the next time he had a run-in with one of the people from his company's corporate office. I'd never seen Brian act like a hothead, but I had personally observed a couple of co-workers who quit on the spot when they didn't like what the boss said. So I knew such things happened.

Of course, that was back during my college days when I was working part-time in a department store while going to school. Even though I told myself Brian wasn't likely to do something impulsive, especially since I knew how much he liked his job, I couldn't help worrying.

I stewed over Brian's situation for a while until Laddie jumped up and nudged my arm with his nose, reminding me that it was time for him to go outside before bedtime. There was a full moon so I could easily see him as he focused his attention on a lizard perched on top of the back wall, ran toward it, and jumped at the wall, his front feet well below where the lizard lay. Although Laddie couldn't reach him, the lizard rapidly disappeared down the other side of the wall. Laddie's burst of energy spent, he wandered around for a while, but I could tell he was tired, and we soon headed for bed.

My mind whirled with thoughts of Emma's displeasure with her father, Brian's problems at work, Rich's murder, and Pamela's arrest. I thought about whether we'd learn anything that would help crack the case tomorrow during our visit to Phoenix. When I finally did go to sleep, I dreamed about my encounter with the Brambles at the grocery store.

Awakening, I shuddered at the thought that Rich's killer could be much closer to home than I'd imagined and sincerely hoped that our trip to Phoenix wasn't going to be in vain.

Chapter 34

Since Emma had to work and wouldn't be home, Susan had volunteered to watch Laddie while I was out of town. He was excited to be going on an outing as he jumped into the back seat and I drove to Susan's. He recognized her studio as soon as I pulled into the driveway and bounced around with excitement at seeing my friend.

"It'll be nice to have a furry companion for the day," Susan assured me when I thanked her for taking care of Laddie. "I'll walk him around the neighborhood, and then I'll work in the studio for a while. I put some blankets down for him in there."

"Perfect. He'll love it, and he'll settle right down while you're working. At least, he does at home."

"Laddie will be just fine," Susan assured me. "I hope you get to the bottom of Rich's mysterious finances. I just can't imagine what he was thinking to put a mortgage on their house. How could he do that without Pamela's knowledge?"

"I don't know, but it sure doesn't sound good. Of course, she has bigger problems with the charges against her."

"What if it turns out she's bankrupt? She won't even be able to pay for a lawyer!"

"Fingers crossed. I'm hoping she isn't bankrupt, and that her case won't ever go to court. We just have to find out who really did it."

"Well, I wish you luck."

"Thanks. Pamela and I need it!"

After admonishing my retriever to "be a good boy" and giving him a good-bye hug, I jumped into my SUV. I arrived home just in time for Emma to take the car to work.

Pamela wouldn't be coming by to pick me up for another forty-five minutes, so I had plenty of time to get ready. I took a long cotton gauze dress and a linen jacket out of the closet and hung them on the back of the bathroom door while I showered.

Then, I selected my favorite pair of sandals, the ones with cushy memory foam soles, to wear so that I'd be comfortable. I doubted that we'd have to walk very far, but, just in case, I wouldn't have to struggle in high heels in the brutal Phoenix heat.

Pamela pulled up in front of my house right on time. I was surprised when Mona Lisa let out a loud, protesting "mrrrow" as I was closing the front door. Usually, she took little notice of my comings and goings, and she was happy to have the place all to herself when Laddie was gone, too.

As soon as I slipped into the passenger seat, greeted Pamela, and fastened my seat belt, we got underway. There wasn't much traffic in Lonesome Valley as Pamela drove through town, but as soon as we merged onto I-17, we were immediately surrounded by eighteen-wheelers.

Pamela had her work cut out for her as she navigated through the traffic. I'd wanted to ask her what she knew about John Bramble and maybe push her further to find out what secret she and Chip had been hiding, but, obviously, the time wasn't right for either conversation.

Traffic became even heavier as we entered Phoenix, and I noticed Pamela, her jaw clenched, was gripping the steering wheel. I kept quiet so as not to disturb her concentration, and the only sound in the car was the chirpy voice of her phone's GPS, directing her to the turn-off for the hospital.

As soon as we were on surface streets, I noticed that Pamela had relaxed considerably, and we had no trouble finding a parking spot in the lot in front of the hospital.

"Traffic was worse than I expected," Pamela told me as we entered the building.

"It was pretty bad," I agreed.

We headed toward several elevators beyond the reception desk in the lobby and followed a group of hospital workers into the first one that opened.

A white-coated man with a goatee pressed the "4" button. Then, he glanced at Pamela and me, his eyebrows raised, and I said "6, please." He nodded, punched the button for "6," and the elevator doors slid closed.

The entire group got off on the fourth floor, leaving Pamela and me alone in the elevator. She took a deep breath, and I noticed her hands were shaking. I wanted to reassure her that everything would be all right, but I didn't know whether that was the case or not.

"I hope Fred can help," she said in a shaky voice. "I don't really know what to ask him. Would you talk to him?"

"Of course. We've got this," I said with more confidence that I felt. After all, Fred had agreed to our meeting, and he had been Rich's employee, which meant that Pamela was now his boss, and he should certainly cooperate with her.

"Room 612," she whispered as the elevator door opened.

We walked down the hall and found the door to Room 612 halfway open. Pamela knocked on the door frame to signal our arrival.

A man's voice called out, "Come in."

On seeing us, Fred raised himself to a sitting position in the hospital bed, grimacing as he did so. The poor guy looked a fright with big black-and-blue bruises all the way down the right side of his face and his right arm.

Despite knowing about the accident that had landed him in the hospital, I was shocked by his appearance.

Gingerly, he scooted a few inches forward, grunting in pain. "Hello, Pamela. Long time, no see."

Although he attempted a joking tone, he didn't quite pull it off.

"Fred, this is my friend, Amanda."

Fred nodded, and I said hello. It was clearly an effort for him to speak.

"I'm so sorry about your accident!" Pamela exclaimed.

"Not an accident; at least, that's what Cheri tells me. Last thing I remember is getting out of my car at the TV station. I was going to pick up Cheri. Then I woke here, in the hospital, Saturday morning. I guess I'll be able to go home in a couple of days, but I don't know about the office."

"Don't worry about that."

"Oh, but I do. Someone needs to be there. I can do some work from home, but it's hard to concentrate when I'm feeling lousy."

"Of course it is. Can't Sheila Granville take charge while you're out?"

"I guess so. She's next senior after me. It's just that she's not really too familiar with our financials since she's the sales manager. I'll do my very best to get back into the office next week."

"You just take care of yourself. Sheila can always call you, if need be."

"All right, but I should be the one telling you to take of yourself. I still can't believe they're charging you with Rich's murder. That's ridiculous."

"That's one of the reasons we wanted to see you today, Fred," Pamela said. "Amanda?"

"Yes, we were wondering whether someone at the company might have had reason to harm Rich. Had he fired anyone recently or perhaps had a major disagreement with one of the employees?"

Fred frowned. "Only one springs to mind, but you already know all about it, Pamela."

"I have no idea what you're talking about," Pamela said.

"But didn't you sign with Rich to take out a mortgage on your house in Lonesome Valley?"

"If I did, I didn't realize what I was signing. Every once in a while, Rich asked me to sign routine paperwork, but I never read it. He took care of all our finances. He sure never mentioned that I was signing documents to put a mortgage on our house."

So Pamela had signed the mortgage agreement, after all, even though she'd done it inadvertently. I had the feeling she would have gone along with whatever Rich wanted in any case, but, for some reason, he hadn't clued her in on his reasons for putting a mortgage on a house that was almost paid for.

Fred groaned. "So you don't know?"

"Know what?"

"One of our accountants embezzled almost two million dollars from the company. Rich took out the mortgage and sold some stock to put the money back into the company because he was considering an offer we'd had or taking the business public. Actually, he'd decided he really wanted to take it public, but we'd have to stabilize our finances because of the embezzlement before we could do it. He didn't want to bring the police into the matter or let word leak out about what happened."

"What did happen?" I asked.

"We confronted the guy, and he agreed to a repayment deal in exchange for our not reporting the crime."

"When was this?"

"A week ago Friday."

"A couple of days before Rich's murder," I said, "and last Friday, you were run down."

Pamela and I exchanged a look.

"Will may be an embezzler, but he's no murderer," Fred said.

"What makes you say that?" I asked. He certainly sounded like a viable suspect to me. I was sure Pamela thought so, too, by the way she'd gripped my arm when Fred had revealed the embezzlement.

"Well, when we told him we wouldn't go to the police if he agreed to repay what he'd stolen, he seemed relieved. Why rock the boat?"

"Maybe he was angry at being found out. Could be he figured if he got rid of you and Rich, he wouldn't have to pay the money back.

How was he supposed to do that, anyway? You did fire him, didn't you?" I asked.

"Well. . . ."

Pamela gasped. "Don't tell me he's still working for the company."

"Technically, I guess he is."

"You've got to be kidding me," Pamela burst out. "I can't believe this!"

"Wait a minute, Pamela. It's not as crazy as it sounds. Remember, Rich had pretty much decided that he wanted the company to go public, so he thought it was absolutely vital that not a whisper of the embezzlement came to light. We told Will not to come into the office anymore. Our cover story was that he'd be out on medical leave for a few months."

"So R. J. Smith Software is still footing the bill, and I assume he's still drawing a paycheck," Pamela said.

"We had to do it that way; otherwise, people might have started asking questions, and the embezzlement might have come to light."

"Unbelievable!" Pamela's normally pale complexion had turned a deep purplish red. I don't think I'd ever seen her so angry. "How *could* he?" she muttered, more to herself than to Fred and me, and I knew she was talking about her husband, not Will.

"Pamela, Rich was just trying to protect the company," Fred said.

But Pamela wasn't deterred. "Here's what we're going to do," she announced. "We're going to report the embezzlement to the police and press charges, return the cover-up money so that I can pay off my mortgage that I didn't even know I had, and fire Will."

"But we had an agreement."

"I didn't agree to anything," Pamela shouted and stalked out of the room.

I glanced at Fred and told him, "She's serious."

"But. . . ."

"She's the boss now. You'd better get used to it."

Fred's mouth fell open as he looked at me in shock before I turned and hurried out, into the hallway, to catch up to Pamela.

Maybe we were finally getting somewhere.

Chapter 35

By the time I caught up with her, Pamela was pacing in circles in front of the elevators. With her head down, she didn't see a nurse hurriedly approaching, and she nearly collided with her. If the nurse hadn't swerved at the last second, they probably both would have ended up on the floor.

Turning, the nurse snapped, "Watch where you're going!" before continuing on her way.

The rude tone of the comment seemed to bring Pamela to attention. When she noticed me, she grabbed my arm.

"Let's go!" she exclaimed, pulling me toward the elevator.

The packed elevator slowly descended, stopping at every floor along the way. It was no place to have a private discussion, and neither Pamela nor I uttered a word until we left the hospital.

At a rapid pace, Pamela started toward her car.

"Hold on," I said. "What are you going to do?"

"What I *should* have done in the first place. I'm going over to the office to let everyone know who's boss. Fred acts as though *he's* in charge."

Pamela was so angry I could almost picture steam coming out of her ears.

"It did seem that way, but I think he has the message now."

"He'd *better*," Pamela muttered. "I checked our personal bank accounts before I picked you up this morning. I should have looked into them earlier, but I've been too upset about Rich to care much about anything else. Anyway, there's no money at all in our savings account and very little in the checking—not even enough to cover the monthly payment on this stupid mortgage that Rich tricked me into approving. If I don't do something, I'm going to lose the house. I won't be able to pay for a lawyer, either. I'll be stuck with a public defender when my life's on the line."

Pamela's bravado dissolved into sobs as she finished her speech and began crying on my shoulder. I was amazed that she'd been able to cope as long as she had. On the other hand, I was glad she'd finally recognized what a precarious position she was in, although it was understandable that losing Rich had been her sole focus since his murder.

When her sobs finally turned to hiccups, we walked slowly toward her car. A few passersby glanced at her curiously and then looked away, probably thinking that she'd had bad news about a relative in the hospital.

When we reached the car, Pamela dug her car keys out of her bag.

I held out my hand, and she looked at me.

"I'm driving," I announced. "You're in no state to be fighting traffic."

She meekly handed the keys over without a word and climbed into the passenger seat while I took my place behind the wheel and started the engine.

"Home or do you want to go to Rich's office?"

"Rich's office," she said decisively. "I need to get this mess straightened out before things get even worse."

The headquarters of Rich's software company was located in a sprawling maze-like business complex not far from the hospital. If Pamela hadn't been along to guide me, it would have taken me quite a while to locate the right building and suite. At Pamela's direction, I parked in Rich's spot, in a covered parking place to shelter the car from the blazing sunshine.

Inside, there was a large open area with numerous unoccupied desks. I saw only two people at work, but there were several offices along the right side. We found Sheila in the last one; all the others were vacant.

"Where is everybody?" Pamela asked, startling Sheila so much that she jumped and tipped over her coffee cup.

Luckily, it was empty.

"Pamela, I didn't know you were coming in today," Sheila said as she set her cup upright. "Almost everyone's working from home these days."

"Oh, right. That's what Rich was doing, too."

"Come in. Sit down," Sheila urged, clearing a stack of papers from a seat in front of her desk. "I'll be right back." She went next door and brought another chair in, motioning to us to be seated.

After introducing me to Sheila, Pamela got right down to business.

"What can you tell me about Will Garfield?"

Sheila looked confused. "He's out on leave from what Fred told me. Some kind of medical problem I guess."

"So you don't know?"

"Know what?"

"Will embezzled quite a lot of money from the company. I want to file a complaint with the police."

"*Will*? He seems like such a nice guy. I can't believe he'd do such a thing."

"Believe it."

"Does Fred know?"

"Fred's the one who told me about it. By the way, you're in charge, at least until Fred returns. After that, we'll see."

Sheila got the message quicker than Fred had.

"Would you like me to consult our lawyer? To file a complaint with the police, we're going to need evidence. We may have to engage a forensic accountant to put it together."

"Yes; please call the lawyer and set up a meeting as soon as possible. In the meantime, you can get the details from Fred. Now, I'll need a check for ten thousand dollars cut to me right away."

"All right. How should I tell the clerk to account for it?"

"Partial loan repayment."

"Will do. This should only take a couple of minutes. Can I get you anything while you're waiting? Coffee? Water?"

"I'll have a bottle of water, please," I said. "Pamela?"

"Same."

Sheila returned with a couple of bottles of cold water before leaving us alone in her office. I assumed one of the people we saw must be a bookkeeping clerk since, as sales manager, Sheila wouldn't be writing any company checks herself.

"I think we should try to find out where Will Garfield is," I told Pamela.

Before Pamela had a chance to comment, Sheila came back with a frown on her face.

"The bank just called to tell us that a fifty-thousand dollar check written to the company by Will Garfield came back due to insufficient funds."

"All the more reason to find out where he is," I told Pamela. "I doubt that he had any intention of ever repaying any of the money he stole. His agreement to repay was probably just a stalling maneuver. He could have left town by now."

Sheila sat down at her desk and turned to her computer. "I'll try to contact him right now. Will has a mobile number listed in the company directory, no landline."

She punched in the number on the phone on her desk and put the phone on speaker mode. Within seconds, we heard a robotic voice intone, "This number's no longer in service." Sheila hung up. There was no need to wait to hear the rest of the message. Clearly, Will wanted to remain incommunicado.

"What's his address?" I asked Sheila. I figured we'd gone this far, and I wanted to confirm what I suspected: that he'd left Phoenix.

"Are you sure we should go over there?" Pamela asked. "I'm livid at him, but he could be dangerous."

"You're right; he might be dangerous, but I don't think we're going to find him at home. Even if we do, I doubt that he'd try anything in broad daylight. If he's the one who ran Fred down or stabbed Rich in the back, he's the sneaky type."

Turning to Sheila, I asked, "Do you have a picture of him, so we know who we're looking for?"

She was unable to hide her shocked expression as she once again consulted her computer. She turned the screen towards us, and Pamela and I peered at a photo of Will that had appeared in the company newsletter back in March.

"He hasn't changed his hair style or gained a bunch of weight since March, has he?" I asked.

"No, he looks just the same as he did when I saw him last," Sheila responded.

"We'd better get going then," Pamela said. "I'm putting his address in my GPS. Sheila, you'll keep me informed?"

"I certainly will. I'll get in touch with Fred and our lawyer to get the ball rolling."

"All right. Call me as soon as you have a meeting set up."

"I will," Sheila assured her.

We drove to Will's house, which turned out to be in a gated community. I waited at the side of the entry until a resident driving a black Mercedes pulled up to the gate and opened it. Then I followed him into the neighborhood.

When I parked at the curb in front of Will's house, a stocky man with black hair was removing a "For Sale" sign from the front yard. Since the picture we'd seen of Will had shown a slender man with light hair, we knew he wasn't Will.

We stepped out of the car and greeted the man.

"Hello, we're looking for Will Garfield," I said. "Do we have the right address?"

"Oh, you mean the previous owner. We just moved in last week. Thought it was about time to take this sign down. I asked the listing agent to remove it, but he hasn't shown up."

Pamela groaned and murmured, "Oh, no."

"You don't happen to know where Will moved, do you?"

"Nope. Only saw him once, and he mentioned something about taking a long vacation. Maybe his real estate broker would know. Say, if you talk to him, could you tell him that his company's sign is in my garage? If he wants it, he'll have to come by on the weekend."

Pamela nodded although I knew the location of the "For Sale" sign was the furthest thing from her mind.

"Should we check with the broker?" Pamela asked after we climbed back into the car.

"I suppose, but I doubt that Will left a forwarding address."

"What was the name of that company? Do you remember?"

"Uh, let's see. Something with Dale—Dale Knight or Dale Knightly, I think."

Pamela picked up her phone and began searching for the name. I waited to start the car until she found it.

"Here is it. Dale Knightly Real Estate. I'm going to call and ask."

The phone rang a couple of times before a woman answered.

"Dale Knightly, please."

"Just a moment."

Suddenly Pamela's hand began shaking, and she thrust the phone at me. "You talk to him. I'm too nervous."

She'd been holding it together since her meltdown in the hospital parking lot, but in her state of mind, the ups and downs came fast and furious.

I took the phone and waited for Dale.

"Dale Knightly; how may I help you?"

"Mr. Knightly, my name is Amanda Trent. I'm from Lonesome Valley, and I'm trying to get in touch with my cousin Will Garfield. I'm parked in front of his house right now—and I was surprised to find out he'd moved. I usually only see him maybe once a year, you know, at the family's holiday gathering, but I thought since I was here in town for the day, I'd stop by to visit him."

Pamela looked at me in astonishment as I spun my tale. Wondering if he'd refuse my request, citing privacy concerns, I held my breath, but, evidently he had no such qualms because he didn't hesitate to answer.

"Sorry I can't be much help. Will told me he'd let me know his address as soon as he got settled in his new home, but I haven't heard from him."

"But he's still in Phoenix, isn't he? I guess I could check his office."

"You won't find him there. He resigned because he has a new job in Florida. I guess it was kind of sudden because he said he had to move in a hurry."

"Well, thank you anyway."

"No problem. Now if you ever decide to leave Lonesome Valley and move to Phoenix, be sure to get in touch. I'd be happy to show you some great homes here."

"All right. 'Bye now." I disconnected before he decided to expand on his sales pitch.

When I handed her phone back to Pamela, I noticed that the home-owner who'd bought Will's house was staring at us.

"We'd better get going," I said, starting the car.

As we left the community, I could hear my stomach growling. It was so loud that Pamela heard it, too. By this time, it was late afternoon, and neither of us had eaten a thing since Pamela picked me up.

"Would you like to stop for a late lunch?" Pamela asked. "Or maybe we should call it an early dinner at this point."

Although I wanted nothing more than to get home and wind down, I sensed that Pamela wanted to stop, and I couldn't deny that I was hungry. I pulled into a parking lot to call Emma and ask her to pick up Laddie at Susan's house and feed the pets their dinner. She told me she'd pick him up as soon as she left work. Then I texted Susan to let her know that Emma would be by soon and that I'd call her later to fill her in on what we'd found out.

We spotted a small restaurant in the strip mall where I'd parked and settled for it. The food turned out to be mediocre, and we didn't linger.

By the time we arrived back in Lonesome Valley, it was dark outside, and I felt exhausted. It had been a long day. We'd learned a lot, but, although we'd found out about a crime, we hadn't uncovered any evidence that could lead to Rich's killer.

I was beginning to think that Will wasn't the hit-and-run driver who'd injured Fred. After all, I couldn't see that he would have had anything to gain from hurting the Vice-President of R. J. Smith Software, especially since both Fred and Rich had agreed to settle with him, giving him enough time to flee with his ill-gotten gains.

And if Will hadn't had any reason to harm Fred, he had no motive to kill Rich, either.

Chapter 36

It wasn't until I was sipping my morning coffee after I'd made amends with Laddie for leaving him for an entire day by taking him for an extra long walk that I realized I'd turned my cellphone off before we left Phoenix.

Since I hadn't remembered to take it out of my bag when I arrived home, I retrieved it and checked for messages. Although Susan had texted me that she had a meeting to attend and would talk to me later, Brian hadn't called, and his silence worried me because he was in the habit of calling me every evening.

I'd told him that I'd planned to go to Phoenix with Pamela, but I'd also indicated that I'd be back by dinnertime. I wracked my brain trying to remember if I'd promised to call him. I didn't think so, but I wasn't sure.

I hated to call him at work, but it was still early. I thought he probably wouldn't have gone to his office yet, so I decided to give it a go. When he answered the phone, I heard clattering plates and the sound of several voices in the background, and I knew my timing hadn't been the best.

"Hi, Amanda. I can't talk now," Brian whispered. "I'm at a breakfast meeting."

"Oh, I'm sorry. I didn't mean to interrupt you."

"No problem. I'll call you this evening. Talk to you later."

He hung up without waiting for me to say good-bye. At least, he hadn't sounded worried, but he'd certainly rushed to get off the phone, and I felt a little guilty for bothering him when he was working, even though he wouldn't normally be busy this early. I wondered whether the bigwigs from his company's home office had come back to town already, but I figured Brian would fill me in when he called later.

I didn't have time to dwell on speculation about Brian's problems at work because Susan called, eager to find out what Pamela and I had learned in Phoenix.

"It's a long story," I told my friend. "Do you have time to come over now? I'll make us a coffee cake and some strong coffee, and I'll tell you all the gory details."

"Sounds good to me, but I'm actually still in bed. I can be there in about an hour."

"Perfect timing. I'll whip up the coffee cake right now and pop it into the oven."

Early morning was the best time to bake in the summer in Lonesome Valley. The nights cooled off considerably with the low temperature of the day occurring around dawn. I was usually able to turn off my air conditioner for a while in the morning before the house began to warm up, and today was no exception.

It took me only a few minutes to prepare the batter and add my toppings to the coffee cake. I placed it into the oven, set the timer for half an hour, and waited for Emma to finish her shower before I took mine. When I finished, I quickly dressed, towel dried my hair, fluffing it out a bit with my fingertips, and swiped on some eyeliner and lipstick.

When I finished, I found Emma cuddling Mona Lisa and Laddie.

"Mom, is it OK if I borrow the car, or do you need it today?"

Feeling the need to regroup after yesterday's revelations, I hadn't exactly planned my day.

"Go ahead and take it, Emma. I don't think I'll need it, but I can always call for a ride share if I decide to go somewhere."

"Thanks, Mom. Gotta run," she said, disentangling herself from the pets and grabbing the SUV's key from the little china bowl on the kitchen counter where I habitually kept them.

Laddie ran to my side, and I petted him for a few minutes until the timer rang, and I had to shoo him out of the kitchen so that he wouldn't get too close to the stove when I took the coffee cake out of the oven.

Leaving it cooling on a rack on the counter, I set napkins and forks on my dinky table and waited for Susan's arrival. Laddie panted with excitement when he saw her.

"Uh, oh," I warned Susan. "He's about ready to give you a hug."

"Come on, Laddie," she invited, and my golden boy jumped up and put his big paws on her shoulders and she encircled him with her arms. Satisfied with the greeting, he dropped back down, his tail whipping back and forth. "Aw, I missed him. He's a good companion. He didn't give me a bit of grief yesterday."

"He's a happy camper all right. I wish I could say the same for Mona Lisa."

At the mention of her name, my calico kitty let out an ear-splitting yowl, and we both laughed.

"Hmm. She acts like she knows just what you said."

"Sometimes I wonder. Ready for some coffee?"

"Definitely. I don't feel wide awake until after my first cup."

Susan sat at the table while I filled our mugs and cut a couple of generous slices of coffee cake. Carefully lifting them out of the pan with a spatula, I set them on our plates.

"Smells good," Susan commented, taking a bite. "Umm. Still warm and tastes good, too. What *is* that flavor?"

"It's rhubarb."

"Really? I don't think I've ever had it before. I like it, though."

"You won't find it growing around here, but the supermarket has it once in a while. I had a small clump of it in our yard in Kansas City. There was usually enough for a couple of pies every summer. I used some rhubarb jam that my cousin sent me in this coffee cake."

"Yummy!"

While I filled Susan in on the events of the previous day, we sipped our coffee and indulged in a second slice of cake.

"I feel as though we haven't made any progress. Pamela has a real mess on her hands with the problems at Rich's company, and I don't know how that's going to come out. I just hope the business is stable enough to withstand the hit from the embezzlement."

"You don't think they'll be able to recover any of the money?"

"I doubt it. It seems as though Will planned to leave in the first place. I bet he was stringing Rich and Fred along just long enough to collect the funds from the sale of his house. He's probably lounging on some beach in the Caribbean by now."

"There must be something we can do."

"I can think of one thing. I suspect that Pamela and Chip are holding something back. Whatever it is, they've been secretive about it."

Susan groaned. "My nephew's back to flirting with Pamela?"

"I don't think it's so much flirting, more like a confidence between friends."

"Do you want me to ask him what's going on?"

"Yes. I think he's going to be more inclined to confide in you. I've tried to ask him about it, but he avoided answering."

"OK, I'll see what I can find out. How about Pamela?"

"I can talk to her. Actually, I intended to ask her about the confidence and also about John Bramble when we went to Phoenix yesterday, but the time never seemed right, especially after we found out about the embezzlement."

"I can't understand why either Pamela or Chip would hold something back, especially when Pamela's freedom is at stake."

"It does seem odd, and maybe they'll never tell us what the big secret is, but I hope one or the other of them spills. It's possible that they think it's not important."

"Could be. I'm going to have a word with Chip this morning. He's supposed to come over to get some more of his supplies to move them back to his studio above the gallery."

"All right. I'm keeping my fingers crossed that he'll talk to you. In the meantime, I'll call Pamela and arrange to visit her."

As soon as Susan left, I called Pamela at home. Mrs. Bramble answered and told me she'd gone to the Roadrunner and planned to be there all morning. I decided my best bet would be to go to the gallery to talk to her. Her office afforded plenty of privacy, and we weren't likely to be disturbed.

Reaching for my keys on the china bowl on the counter only to find them gone, I remembered that Emma had taken my SUV to work. Wishing I'd thought of that before Susan had left, I called for an Uber.

As soon as I saw it was a minute away, I went to the front curb and waited, thinking about the day that Chip had been my Uber driver and he'd mentioned something cryptic regarding Pamela.

I'd dismissed it as inconsequential at the time. Now I wondered whether or not my assessment had been wrong. Whether Chip's inadvertent words then had anything to do with whatever confidence he and Pamela were sharing, I didn't know. Perhaps one had nothing to do with the other.

Ralph and Frank, a high school art teacher who was also a member of the board of the Roadrunner, were re-arranging some of Ralph's paintings when I arrived, but there were no shoppers in the gallery.

"Hi, Amanda," Frank said. "What's up?"

"Not much, Frank. I'm looking for Pamela."

"She's in her office," Ralph piped up. "I wish she didn't think she has to be here. I've assured her that we can take care of the gallery just fine, but she showed up anyway."

"It might be easier for her to be here than staying home without Rich," I suggested.

Ralph sighed. "Probably so."

He turned back to Frank, and they resumed their work while I went down the hall to Pamela's office. Her door was open, so I walked in to find her studying something on her computer. She looked up when she heard me.

"Good timing, Amanda. I was going to call you in a few minutes. Have a seat."

"Any word from Sheila?" I asked.

"We're having a videoconference this afternoon with the company lawyer. Fred has his laptop now, so he's going to join in from his hospital bed. I talked to him this morning, and he said he's feeling a little better. According to his doctor, he'll probably be discharged from the hospital tomorrow. He insists he'll be able to come back to the office next week, but I guess we'll have to see about that."

"Did you two patch things up? Things got tense there right before we left."

"Nobody apologized, but Fred seems to have accepted that he's going to have to deal with me now that Rich is gone. Also, he now understands that Will was just buying time when he agreed to the repayment plan. When Sheila told him about Will's check being returned from the bank, and I informed him that Will sold his house and left town, the truth finally sank in. I bet he feels like a fool to have fallen for Will's nonsense, but I guess I can't blame him too much since he was following the boss's lead. Honestly, I don't know what Rich was thinking. He usually wasn't so gullible."

"He must have been focused on his plans for the company and figuring out how to take it public after the hit from the embezzlement.

"Yes. I think you're right. Fred did say that Rich preferred going public to selling out. The business was always his baby, and he never expressed any desire to do anything else."

"Do you want to do that?"

"I doubt that going public is a viable option now. Anyway, I have no interest in running the company or worrying about the software business. Rich loved it, but it's just not my thing. If there was a chance to sell, I'd probably take it."

I nodded. I could certainly understand how Pamela felt. Her main interests centered around her artwork and the gallery. Although I hated to bring up an even sorer subject than the issues at Rich's company, I'd come to the gallery to find out what I could from Pamela. I decided to ease into it by first inquiring about her housekeeper's husband before I brought up the subject of the secret that Pamela and Chip shared.

"Uh, Pamela, what can you tell me about John Bramble?"

"John?" She looked at me in surprise. "Not much really. I've met him a few times, and his wife's told me about his many health issues. Other than that, I don't know."

"Oh," I said, disappointed. I'd hoped that Pamela knew more about the man than I did.

"Surely you don't suspect him. With his back problems, I doubt that he'd be out and about. I think he stays home most of the time except for medical appointments."

"I saw him at the supermarket, and he didn't show any signs of distress."

"Mrs. Bramble tells me his pain can be excruciating sometimes. Maybe he was having a good day."

"I guess so." Perhaps my impression of John Bramble as being something of a malingerer had been off-base. I wished I could find another way to confirm his condition, but, of course, any medical records would be protected by privacy laws. I wondered how thoroughly the police had checked the Brambles' alibis for the day Rich was killed.

Lieutenant Belmont probably wouldn't be in any mood to share that information, and Dave hadn't been too forthcoming lately either.

"He never had words with Rich, by any chance, did he?"

"Not that I can recall. I'm sure he wasn't happy when he found out Rich wanted to fire his wife, especially because they would have lost their medical insurance. I wouldn't have let that happen, though."

"Hmm. Well, I thought I'd check. Pamela, there's something else I need to ask you." I hesitated. "What are you and Chip hiding?"

Chapter 37

Flabbergasted at my blunt question, Pamela stared at me and declared, "Nothing. We're not hiding anything."

"Look, Pamela, I don't care whether Chip wants to get back together with you."

"Don't be ridiculous! I can't imagine why you would even suggest such a thing. Rich hasn't even been buried yet." She began to cry.

I felt terrible for having been the cause of her current distress, but, if we couldn't figure out who killed Rich, she'd be in a far worse predicament than she was now.

"I'm sorry to have to ask, Pamela, but it could be important to your case. You can't deny that you and Chip have some kind of secret. If it isn't your relationship with him, then what is it?"

Pamela dabbed her face with a couple of tissues and rubbed her hand across her forehead.

"You won't quit until I tell you, I suppose."

I didn't respond. I figured if I remained silent, she might go on. I crossed my arms and waited.

"All right. I'll tell you, but it's not going to affect my case one way or the other. I'm sure of that."

"Go on."

"Chip lied to the police. He told Lieutenant Belmont that the last time he saw Rich was early Sunday afternoon. Actually, it was later in the day."

"Why didn't he say so?"

"I suppose he thought the lieutenant would consider him a suspect if he admitted he'd seen Rich closer to the time I found him, especially if he'd revealed that he saw Rich slash his painting."

"But Chip suggested as much to the lieutenant, although, if I remember right, he made it seem like speculation. Did he say where Rich went after he cut the painting?"

"No. Chip was angry, but he didn't want to get into a confrontation because Rich had a knife, so he turned around and went back to his booth. Rich never saw him, and nobody else did either, according to Chip."

"So you believe Chip?"

"Yes, I do. He didn't have to tell me, either, you know. He said he'd go to the police with the information if that's what I wanted, but neither of us figured Rich's slashing the painting would help my case at all. In fact, it might make me look more suspicious."

"Why do you think so?"

"Because I was so put out with Rich that day that I said something I shouldn't have. We'd had a big argument before going to the park, and I was still really angry with him for wanting to let Mary go. After we got the Roadrunner's booth set up, Rich left to get breakfast, and Chip came over to talk to me. That's when I said it."

"What did you say?"

"I said that I felt so angry I could just kill Rich. You have to understand I didn't really mean it, Amanda, but I never should have spouted off, and if I'd known Rich slashed the painting Chip gave me, I would have been even madder. Saying what I did makes me sound guilty, as though I really wanted my husband dead, which, of course, I absolutely did not!"

Tears sprang to Pamela's eyes, and she reached for the box of tissues for the second time since I'd visited her this morning. "I feel terrible that I ever said such a thing. I feel even worse that Rich and I never really made up, and we were sniping at each other all day. When it came time to close and pack up the Roadrunner's booth and he wasn't around to help, I felt beyond annoyed. So our last day together was horrible. Our last words to each other were spiteful, not loving. I'll never forgive myself."

"Try not to dwell on the unpleasantness, Pamela. The fact is that you loved Rich, and he knew it."

"I did. Very much. Oh, why couldn't the cops understand that I never would have done anything to harm him?"

"I'm afraid the chief wanted a quick resolution to a murder case." Although I didn't tell Pamela, I thought that if Lieutenant Belmont hadn't been pressured into arresting her, Pamela would probably still be a free woman, rather than a murder suspect out on bail. I wondered whether the police were still involved in gathering evidence, but I was sure Lieutenant Belmont wouldn't discuss the case with me, not after my promise to "stand down" if Nate didn't turn out to be the killer.

Although my chat with Pamela had revealed new information that didn't put either Pamela or Chip in the best light, I didn't believe for a moment that they could have been involved in Rich's murder. I was no closer to finding out who'd stabbed Rich than I had been before I'd talked with Pamela.

As I exited the gallery, Susan rang me to let me know what she'd managed to wheedle out of Chip. His story matched Pamela's, which was no surprise. I was running out of ideas when Susan came up with a plan.

"Maybe we should look into John Bramble more," she suggested. "We really haven't learned much of anything about him."

"What do you have in mind?" I asked. "I've checked his social media account, and he's on only one platform, as far as I can tell. Pamela couldn't shed any light on him, so all we basically know is that he's supposed to be some sort of an invalid since his back surgery. I have to say he certainly didn't seem like one when I saw him and his wife at the supermarket, but, like Pamela said, maybe he was having a good day."

"How about a stakeout? Maybe we can get a better idea about his condition."

"Seriously?"

"Sure; why not? We'll cruise by his house first, and then maybe watch it this evening."

"What if they recognize the car? We've both been to Pamela's house plenty of times."

"I was about to say we could borrow Chip's, but I had a momentary lapse there and forgot he has that new red car. That won't do for a stakeout."

I couldn't help giggling at our somewhat absurd conversation. Nevertheless, I was about to get on board with Susan's plan.

"I know!" Susan said. "I'll borrow my brother's pickup for the evening. I'm sure he won't mind."

"All right."

"Why don't you meet me, and we'll do a drive-by to get the lay of the land and see where we should park tonight."

"Emma took my SUV to work. Could you pick me up downtown?"

"Sure, but it'll be about an hour. I have a customer coming over to pick up one of my sculptures. Do you want to wait at the gallery?"

"No, I've upset Pamela enough for one day. I think I'll go over to the Bread Bowl and pick up up a loaf of rye. Maybe have a cup of coffee while I'm waiting."

"Good. I'll text you when I leave the house."

As we were talking, I'd stepped into a shady alcove a few doors down from the Roadrunner since I didn't want to stand in front of the gallery discussing Pamela's problems. Now that I'd have a four-block walk to the Bread Bowl, I pulled my sunglasses out of my bag and slipped them on, wishing I'd brought my summer straw hat with me to keep the blazing sunlight off my face.

By the time I reached the bustling restaurant, I was ready to step into the cool air conditioning. The place had a seat-yourself policy, so I found a small booth near the back and sat down. When the server showed up a few minutes later offering a menu, I told her I was just having a drink, but since I'd already had plenty of coffee, I decided to forgo more in favor of a tall glass of iced tea. I certainly didn't need anything else to eat after having consumed two pieces of coffee cake earlier.

Killing time, I sipped my iced tea slowly and then ordered another glass along with a loaf of rye bread to take home. Checking the time, I continued dawdling over the second glass of tea. It would still be a while before Susan could pick me up.

The booth next to me had been vacant when I'd arrived, but now a couple made their way to the back, towards it. As soon as I saw who it was, I turned my head, scrunching down in my seat a bit, pretending to search for something in my purse.

I hadn't said hello to Pamela's brother Nate because I didn't feel like discussing her case with him right at the moment since a woman was with him who may or may not have known that his sister had been arrested and charged with murdering her husband.

As Nate and his companion, an attractive woman in her mid-thirties, settled themselves in the booth next to me, I could hear them talking. Despite the high seat backs, sound traveled due to a gap between the booths and the wall. As they discussed the menu, I tried to tune them out, but when Nate mentioned the word "alibi," my ears perked up and I inched closer to the gap between the booths so that I could hear better.

"I don't think I should have done it," the woman said. "The cops asked me to verify my story again. Why would they do that?"

"You didn't change it, did you, Lynn?"

"No, but. . . ."

"Look. You know me. You know I wouldn't do anything to hurt Pamela. I didn't much care for Rich, but my sister did."

"I'm not accusing you. It's just that I could get in trouble for lying to the police."

"They're never going to know now, are they?"

After several seconds of silence, Nate spoke again.

"Lynn? Come on; tell me you're not considering telling them I wasn't at your house last Sunday afternoon."

"I don't know what I should do. I could be in big trouble here. Don't you care about *me*?"

"Of course I do, honey. You need to stop worrying about it. The cops are never going to find out unless you tell them, and you're not going to do that."

Wondering whether Nate's last words were a veiled threat or a hope, I leaned even closer to the gap, almost knocking my purse off the seat. Thankfully, I grabbed it just in time.

I realized I wouldn't be able to leave until they did; otherwise, Nate might notice me, and I definitely didn't want that to happen now that I'd overheard his girlfriend admit that she'd lied to the police about Nate's whereabouts at the time Rich was murdered. Evidently, his so-called air-tight alibi was nothing but a smoke screen. I wondered where he'd really been if he hadn't been with Lynn that day.

More questions came to mind. Why had Lynn been described as a customer when she was really Nate's girlfriend? Hadn't Nate's dispatcher also told the police he'd been out on a job? Could Nate have killed Rich, just as I'd initially thought?

Pulling my cellphone out of my bag, I was about to let Susan know when I noticed that she'd texted me that her buyer was running late, so she was, too.

I tensed as my server approached, and I waved her off, pointing to my glass, which was still half full. I wasn't sure Nate would recognize my voice, but I didn't want to say a word in case he did.

Luckily, Nate and his girlfriend didn't linger. Shortly after they had coffee and split a sweet roll, they left, and I breathed a huge sigh of relief. It seemed as though everyone kept secrets, and Nate was no exception. I knew I should go to Lieutenant Belmont and tell him what I'd learned, but I also realized that he wouldn't want to listen to anything I had to say, not after he'd decided that Nate wasn't a suspect.

Of course, in my mind Pamela's brother was back on the list, although I had to admit that his declaration that he'd never do anything to hurt his sister certainly seemed to ring true. Then again, maybe he was an accomplished liar. I didn't know him well enough myself to make that determination.

As soon as my server delivered my loaf of bread and the check, I left a tip on the table and went up front to pay at the cash register near the front door. Susan had called to say that she was on the way shortly after Nate and his girlfriend had departed.

Just after I'd gone out front to wait for her, she pulled up, double parking long enough so that I could jump into her car.

"Something smells good," she said. "Rye?"

"Umm, hmm. I'm sorry. I should have asked you if you wanted me to pick up a loaf for you. We can split this one, though."

"No, thanks, Amanda. I have plenty of bread at home. I'd have to freeze it, and bread just doesn't taste as good after it's been frozen."

"That's for sure. So which way are we headed?"

"I looked up the Brambles' address, and their house isn't too far from here, up toward Lookout Hill. We'll take a quick pass by it and, hopefully, we'll be able to scope out a spot where we can watch the house this evening."

"OK. Believe it or not, it's looking like Nate may be back in the frame."

"You're kidding."

"No. He came into the Bread Bowl while I was there." I proceeded to relate Nate's conversation with his girlfriend.

"So we may be spinning our wheels checking out John Bramble."

"Maybe. Oh, I don't know. It feels like we're running around in circles. We might as well go ahead with our surveillance, I suppose."

"We're almost there. We turn left at the next street."

After Susan turned onto Lookout Lane, she drove three blocks.

"Coming up on the right," she said. "Second house from the corner."

We weren't going very fast, but Susan slowed down a bit anyway so that we could get a good look at the small stucco house, which, like the others on the block, had probably had been built sometime in the eighties. The front yard was covered with gravel, bushes grew next to the house, and three tall palm trees stood in a line near the curb. Nothing really stood out except that Lookout Hill rose rather steeply in back of the houses on the right side of Lookout Lane.

"Is there a road up there?" I asked Susan, pointing to the hill.

"Let's take a peek."

She drove about half a mile down the lane, and we turned right on a side street. As we rounded a bend, curving back in the direction we'd come, the road quickly steepened, and we soon found ourselves in back of the houses along Lookout Lane. There were no residences along the way, and the view into the backyards of the houses below was perfect. The only problem was that the road was very narrow.

"No shoulders," Susan commented. "Oh, wait, up there; I see a turnout."

Susan pulled off the road and parked. We were about half a block from the Brambles' house, but since it was doubtful we'd be able to park any closer, we got out of the car and hiked up the road until we were in back of their house.

We peered down into their backyard. A few sagging lawn chairs were scattered about the cement patio, and there was a picnic table on one side, next to a gas grill. Rather than gravel, the backyard was covered with scrubby grass, and a badminton net had been set up in the middle of the lawn.

"What do you think?" Susan asked.

"This is a perfect spot for a stakeout. We don't even need binoculars."

"I doubt that anyone below would look up, but, just in case, we can plant ourselves behind that big bush over there."

I grinned at Susan's pun. "We could bring our own lawn chairs."

"And a picnic."

"I'll bring cookies and make some sandwiches. You're going to have some rye bread, after all. Chicken salad all right?"

"Sure. I love your chicken salad. I'll bring some crunchy veggies and drinks. I'd make potato salad, but it might be too messy."

"It might. We'll stick to finger food."

"What time do you think we should come back?" I asked as we trudged back to Susan's car.

"Definitely before dark. Maybe around seven."

"Why don't I pick you up at quarter till," I suggested. "You don't need to borrow your brother's car, after all. They'll never see my SUV up here."

Our plan made, we spent the rest of the time on the ride back to my house discussing the chances of any of the Brambles coming out to their backyard this evening. The citizens of Lonesome Valley fell into two camps when it came to outdoor activities, and I thought that about half of them left the air-conditioned comfort of their homes only to go to work or run errands, while the other half enjoyed their backyards and liked to use them when the weather permitted.

When Emma came home from work, I let her know that I planned to go out with Susan, so I needed my SUV. Since Matt would be working late, she planned to spend the evening at home with Mona Lisa and Laddie for company.

"Where are you and Susan going for dinner?" Emma asked.

"We're having a picnic. I'm making some chicken salad, and I'm taking sandwiches and cookies."

"Have fun, I'll heat up that leftover pizza for dinner."

I was a bit surprised that Emma hadn't sensed that something was up, but I was glad that she hadn't. I felt confident that we weren't veering into a danger zone with our stakeout, and I didn't want Emma to worry about me or give me another warning to be careful.

Later, when I left to pick up Susan, Emma was watching a movie with Mona Lisa plopped on her lap and Laddie lying at her feet.

Carrying a backpack, Susan came out of her house as soon as I pulled up in front.

"I thought about bringing a couple of aluminum folding chairs," she said, "but I decided we probably didn't want to lug them up to our spot. We can take turns sitting on that big rock we saw."

Ten minutes later, I'd parked on the turnout, and we were walking up the hill. Other than a toddler and his mother playing in one back-yard, we didn't see anyone as we made our way toward our destination in back of the Brambles' house. Although we hadn't spotted any other vehicles on the narrow road earlier in the day, I figured it must get some use. If somebody drove by this evening, we could always pretend that we were out for a hike, though.

When we reached our lookout, we both sat behind a bush on the rock, which turned out to be bigger than we'd remembered. We could easily look down into the Brambles' backyard through the branches, but they wouldn't likely spot us unless we'd moved from our perch at the exact moment they looked up at the hillside. Since there was no activity in their backyard, we ate our picnic dinner, careful to keep our voices down when we spoke.

After about half an hour, a boy and girl, who both appeared to be in their early teens, emerged, each carrying a badminton racket. The girl reached into a container that sat on the picnic table and pulled out a shuttlecock. The two batted it back and forth over the net for a while. From where we were sitting, we could hear them counting each time one of them hit the feathered flyer. Evidently they wanted to see how many times they could hit it, rather than play a game of badminton.

I'd just finished eating a sugar cookie when my phone chimed. I saw that Brian was calling, so I picked up before it made any more noise. Looking down into the Brambles' yard, I felt relieved that the kids evidently hadn't heard anything, as they continued their counting.

"Hi," I whispered.

"Amanda? What's wrong? Are you sick?"

"No. I'm fine."

"I can barely hear you. Can you speak up?"

"Sorry, Brian. I'm trying to keep my voice down. I don't want to be heard."

"What's going on, Amanda?"

"Oh, Susan and I are trying to keep tabs on a suspect, and we don't want him to find out. We're on a stakeout." I couldn't help giggling.

"Are you crazy? That could be dangerous! You need to get out of there right now!"

"I assure you we're safe," I said, somewhat taken aback by his commands.

"You can't possibly know that," he countered. "You said you're watching a suspect. What if he's the killer? Then what? Honestly, Amanda, you need to think about what you're doing."

"I'm not sure I like your tone. I *am* an adult, you know."

"Well, you sure don't act like one sometimes."

"I think I'd better go. I'll call you later after I get home."

"Don't bother!"

As he disconnected, I looked at my phone in surprise.

"Hmm. I wonder what set him off," I said. "Brian's never acted that way toward me before."

"He certainly sounded short-tempered on the phone, but you said he's been having problems at work. Maybe they're getting to him."

"I guess that could be it. I'm kind of flabbergasted that he hung up on me, though."

"Rude. Even if he was having a bad day, he shouldn't have taken it out on you."

I shrugged. "Oh, well. All I can do is call him back later, but since he told me not to bother, maybe it would be better to wait until tomorrow, when he's cooled off."

We turned our attention back to the Bramble kids. After a previous long volley of eighty-three stokes, they'd reached a hundred and were still counting. Then we heard a distant rumble of thunder, and felt a few raindrops splash on our heads. Within seconds, rain began pouring down, and the kids ran inside, taking their equipment with them.

"I guess that's it for our stakeout," Susan proclaimed. "We're going to be drenched by the time we get back to your car."

I quickly stowed our empty bottles and storage containers in a small trash bag, grabbed it, and started walking back down the road with Susan. It was close to dusk, so normally there still would have been plenty of light, but the dark clouds made it quite gloomy.

Susan pulled her phone out of her backpack, turned on the flashlight, and shone it on the lane as we hurried back toward the car. Rivulets of water flowing down the hill onto the road merged into torrents, and we were forced to walk in ankle deep water in places.

It took us twice as long to walk back to the car as it had to reach our stakeout spot earlier. We jumped into my SUV, but before we could fasten our seat belts, we felt something.

A slight bump.

Followed by a bigger jolt.

The car had definitely moved.

"Get out!" we yelled simultaneously.

Chapter 38

Susan and I looked at each other and scrambled to exit the car as the right rear wheel sank into mud beneath the rushing water.

"Oh, no," I groaned when we were back on the road. "I hope the bank doesn't give way, or the car's going to end up in someone's backyard."

"At least *we* won't be in it," Susan said. "That's a relief, anyway. I was scared out of my wits when I felt the car move."

"Me, too," I admitted.

Shaking, we stood staring at the slowly sinking wheel, but after several seconds, it stopped moving.

Despite the heavy rain which continued to pound us, we both realized that things could have been a lot worse.

"I'm calling Triple A," I told Susan. "Hopefully, they can tow the car out of there."

I dug my cellphone and membership card out of my pocket, held it a couple inches from my face so that I could see what I was doing, and jabbed the road service's phone number on my contacts list.

I opted out of their phone system prompts and explained our predicament to a human being, who promised help was on the way but informed me that it would probably be half an hour before the tow truck arrived. The dispatcher promised I'd receive text updates.

"Maybe we should walk back down the hill," Susan said. "We're going to be drenched either way, and there's no shelter up here."

"Except in the car, but there's no way we should chance getting back in it now. Sure, we might as well start walking. We can flag down the tow truck when it comes. They'll let me know when it's on the way, and we can watch for it."

Clinging to each other for support each time we had to forge a stream rushing downhill across the road, we made slow progress down the hill. When we reached the bottom, we noticed that the first house on our left had a wide covered front porch.

"Maybe we could wait on their porch," Susan suggested. "Let's ring the doorbell and ask."

"OK. It would be nice to get out of this rain for a while."

As we approached the porch, we were suddenly greeted by a bright light shining in our eyes.

"Well, if it isn't the dynamic duo," a familiar voice said. "What are you standing there for? Come on up here, out of the rain."

Lieutenant Belmont lowered his weighty flashlight and shined it on the stairs so that we could see our way. I'd had no idea where the lieutenant lived. Although I was surprised to see him, I was happy to get out of the heavy rain. I knew Susan couldn't be too thrilled about unexpectedly encountering the lieutenant, though.

"Good grief! You two look like a pair of drowned.... Never mind; I'll be right back."

He went inside and came back out, carrying a stack of bath towels, which he set on a white wicker chair.

"Help yourselves," he invited.

"Thank you," I said as I dried myself as best I could and wrapped a towel around my head to dry my wet hair while Susan did the same.

Despite her dislike of the lieutenant, Susan murmured her thanks, too.

"So what's the story?"

"We were out for a hike up on hill when it started raining," I said. "By the time we got back to the car, it was stuck in the mud."

"I don't suppose your little jaunt took you in back of the Brambles' house."

"What if it did? We were on a public road," Susan said.

"Uh, huh."

"Besides, we didn't see anything," Susan assured him.

He turned to me. "When will you ever learn? You promised you wouldn't interfere if it turned out that Nate wasn't the killer."

"Speaking of Nate. . . ." I began, ignoring his question.

The lieutenant groaned.

"This could be important," I insisted.

"All right. Out with it."

While he listened, scowling the entire time, I described the conversation between Nate and his girlfriend that I'd overheard at the Bread Bowl earlier.

"You should have told me immediately," he scolded.

"I know. I figured you wouldn't want to talk to me, but I was going to tell you tomorrow, anyway."

My phone beeped with a new text message.

"The tow truck's on the way. We need to go out there to flag it down," I said, pointing to the street in front of the house.

"I'll do it," the lieutenant said. "You two stay put. Where's your car?"

"On the first turnout."

He extended his hand. "Keys."

I dropped my car keys into his hand, along with my Triple A membership card, and we watched as he backed his own car out of the driveway, turned on the police lights on top, and blocked the street. There'd be no way the tow truck could miss him.

When it arrived, the driver jumped out of the cab and talked to the lieutenant before he pulled his car back into the driveway and joined the driver in the tow truck.

"We might as well sit down," Susan said, as we watched the tail lights disappear around the curve leading up the hill. "I can't believe we ran into Belmont of all people. Grrr."

Although I could understand Susan's feelings, I didn't share them. Instead, I was relieved to have been able to tell him about Nate's phony alibi, which I felt confident he'd investigate.

While we waited, I texted Emma to let her know we'd been caught in the downpour and had to have my SUV pulled out of the mud but that I should be home soon.

"Looks like the rain's finally letting up," Susan commented. "I hope the storm completely blows over, and it clears up."

"Me, too. Laddie and Mona Lisa hate the thunder," I said, as headlights appeared down the street, coming our way. "There's the lieutenant with our ride."

He turned into the driveway and parked behind his own car. We draped our wet towels over the wicker furniture on the porch and dashed through the rain to my car.

"Thank you!"

A grunt was his reply, but when he opened the door for me, he said, "Stay out of trouble." He closed it before I could answer, although we both knew it was unlikely that I'd take his admonition to heart.

By the time we reached Susan's house, the rain had lightened to a sprinkle.

"Sorry we ran into Belmont," she said, grabbing her backpack, "but I'm even sorrier we didn't learn a thing at our stakeout."

"I know. We were lucky we didn't end up tumbling down the hill. Now that Nate admitted his alibi was fake, I'm wondering whether he really did stab Rich."

"It could be you were right in the first place."

"I'd hate for it to be Nate, though. You know, for Pamela's sake."

"That's true, too. I don't think we should give up on John Bramble just yet."

"Probably not. Maybe we can figure another angle to work. I'm fresh out of ideas right at the moment, maybe because I'm just too tired to think straight."

"So am I. We'll have to regroup tomorrow," Susan said as she extracted her house key from her backpack.

"OK," I agreed, shivering as a little rivulet of water dripped down my back. I was eager to go home and dry off.

I watched as Susan made her way up the front sidewalk, opened her door, and turned to give me a little wave. As soon as she closed the door, I continued on my way.

By the time I reached home, the storm had blown over, and an enthusiastic greeting from Laddie made me feel better. It was a good thing I didn't have to depend on Mona Lisa for a greeting because she took one look at me, turned around, and jumped onto Emma's lap. When my daughter saw me, she pointed at her cellphone, and I knew she was talking to Matt, so I headed to my bedroom.

While Laddie waited patiently for me, I took a quick shower, put on some light cotton pajamas, and dried my hair with my blow dryer. Even though I usually preferred to air dry my hair, I'd had quite enough of dampness for one day.

Before we went to bed, I took Laddie out to the backyard for a few minutes. Since my patio wasn't covered, the cushioned chairs were wet, and there were a few puddles of standing water, which I swept off the patio with a wide broom while I waited for Laddie.

When we went back inside, I saw that Emma was still talking to Matt, so I put my hands together on my cheek, turning my head to the left and closing my eyes to motion that I was going to bed now. She nodded and gave me a thumbs-up signal.

After I brushed my teeth, I picked up my cellphone from the dresser where I'd deposited it after drying it with a thick hand towel when I came home. It seemed no worse for the soaking it had been through. If I remembered, I usually turned it off before I went to bed. Before I zapped it off, I quickly swiped across the screen to check whether I'd missed any calls or text messages.

When I saw Brian's text, my breath caught. I hesitated before looking at his text, hoping he hadn't followed his hang-up with an unpleasant message. Fortunately, I discovered that it was just the opposite. He offered a profuse apology, saying that he didn't know what had gotten into him and promising that he'd never hang up on me again. He added that he hoped I could forgive him and we were still on for the weekend, ending with a smiley face emoticon.

My inclination was to reply immediately in the affirmative, but then I stopped, wondering whether that was a good idea or not. Since I was woefully out of practice on best dating strategies, I wasn't sure. Finally, I decided I might as well answer him because I knew I was willing to let the incident go. I waited a few minutes to see whether or not he'd respond, but when he didn't, I figured he'd probably already turned in for the night, so I did the same. I knew we could talk the next day.

However, remembering the sting of his earlier words telling me not to "bother" calling him, I decided to let *him* do the calling.

Chapter 39

Luckily, my decision to wait for Brian to call me turned out to be the right one. While I was walking Laddie just after dawn, he called, apologizing again, even though I'd already accepted his apology when I'd texted him the previous evening. Although he hadn't changed his mind about driving home to Lonesome Valley after work Friday afternoon, he promised to be back by mid-morning Saturday so that we could spend the day together.

"Looks like we're back on track," I murmured as I slipped my cellphone into the pocket of my jeans.

Panting, Laddie looked up at me with his big brown eyes as though he understood exactly what I was talking about. He brushed his head against my leg, and I patted his side.

As we circled our little neighborhood park, I thought about what our next move should be to find Rich's killer. I'd been serious when I'd told Susan that I was fresh out of ideas, so I was hoping she'd come up with a new angle for us to investigate. I also wondered what the lieutenant might find out about Nate's alibi or lack of one, but I knew he'd never share any information that he uncovered with me.

After a couple of turns around the park, we walked home at such a brisk pace that we were both out of breath by the time we turned onto

Canyon Drive, but when I saw Emma, ready for work, standing at the curb. I waved, and we stepped up our pace even more.

"Up and dressed already," I said. "I thought Laddie and I were the only early birds around here."

"Ha, ha. I left you a note in case you weren't back from your walk yet before I left. Matt's picking me up. We're going out to breakfast at the Bread Bowl before work."

"Good thing you're going now. You'll beat the rush. They're crazy busy at breakfast. Do you have plans for this evening, too?"

"Just work. We're going to be shorthanded at the store today, so I told Matt I'd work all day until closing. Oh, here he comes now."

Matt pulled up to the curb, got out of his car, greeted me, ruffled Laddie's fur, and opened the passenger door for Emma.

"Have a good breakfast," I told them before he closed the door.

"Thanks, Ms. Trent. We will!" Matt replied.

I'd asked him to call me Amanda a time or two, but perhaps he wasn't comfortable doing it yet, so I didn't remind him again. I made a mental note to check with Emma in hopes that she could persuade him to drop the formality.

After they left, I dawdled over coffee and toast before feeding Laddie and Mona Lisa. Susan wouldn't be up yet, and I knew she usually had a couple of private students who came to her studio for lessons in watercolor techniques on Thursday mornings, so I didn't expect to hear from her until later, anyway. After a round of fetch with Laddie and some playtime with Mona Lisa and her feather toy, I decided I should get to work.

Since I liked to have more than one painting in progress, I underpainted a gessoed canvas in preparation for starting one of my signature abstract landscapes. Then I returned to the landscape that I'd previously been painting and worked on it for a few hours before wrapping up.

I tidied up the place so that it would look presentable for my open studio the next evening. I carefully moved Betsy's portrait, which was sitting on an easel, to the corner behind my desk so that people would be able to see it, but they wouldn't be able to touch it. Then I dusted the room and straightened all the completed canvases that hung on the walls. Laddie stayed in the studio with me until I pulled the vacuum cleaner out of the studio's supply closet. He took one look at it and retreated to the house. Since he hated the vacuum's noise, I closed the door between the studio and living room before I turned the machine on. After emptying the debris into a trash bag and disposing of it, I stowed the vaccum cleaner in the supply closet, opened the door, and called Laddie, who'd been hiding behind a chair in the living room.

"All done, Laddie," I assured him and he ran to me, tail wagging, just as Susan called. I sat down at my desk, my phone in my right hand while I petted Laddie with my left since I knew he wouldn't be denied.

"My second student didn't show up or bother to call," Susan complained. "I think I'm about ready to cut her loose. I waited the entire hour, just in case she came late. I even tried to call her, but she didn't answer. This isn't the first time it's happened, either."

"Any new ideas?" I asked, after commiserating with Susan about her flakey student.

"Not a one."

"Me, either."

"Let's get together and talk it out. Surely two heads are better than one. Why don't you come over? We can discuss where to go from here over lunch. Bring Laddie, too. I miss him!"

"OK, good. Laddie's always up for a visit."

"Come around to the studio when you get here. I'll be re-arranging some of my watercolors."

"Will do."

Sensing that something was up, Laddie pranced around me while I swiped on some lipstick and exchanged my paint-spattered t-shirt for a blue cotton gauze tunic. As soon as I picked up my purse and grabbed my car keys, he ran to his leash, which I'd left draped over the kitchen door handle when we'd returned from his morning walk, and waited patiently while I snapped it on.

My SUV badly needed a bath after the previous night's adventure, but I didn't want to subject Laddie to an automatic wash, so I resolved to take the car later, when he wasn't along for the ride.

When I pulled into Susan's driveway, Laddie began to pant with excitement. He knew just where he was. As soon as I opened the car door, I grabbed his leash, and he jumped out and headed for Susan's front door.

"This way, Laddie," I told him, pulling on his leash so that we could go around the house to Susan's backyard studio.

Susan, who'd heard us coming, opened the studio door and held her arms out for Laddie. He rushed to her, and she gave him a big hug. After their greeting, he began sniffing at her pocket, and she took out a dog biscuit.

"Sit," she commanded, and he promptly obeyed, but his eyes never left the treat.

"Good boy!" she told him, handing him the snack and motioning us to come into the studio.

As we walked inside, our phones simultaneously went off. We looked at each other and grinned at what we thought was a coincidence, but our smiles turned to frowns when we learned that both Ralph and Dawn had been trying to reach Pamela all morning, and their calls had gone unanswered.

"We're getting concerned," Dawn told me. "Of course, there could be an explanation, but Pamela told Ralph that she'd be in this morning to make next month's schedule, but she hasn't called and, since we can't get a hold of her. . . ."

"Say no more. Susan and I can go over to her house right now to check on her."

"Thank you! That would be great. You'll let us know then?"

"I'll call you when we get there. Maybe she just needed some peace and quiet for a few hours, but I admit it's not like Pamela. Still, with everything she's gone through lately, you never know."

Susan assured Ralph that we were on our way to Pamela's house, too.

"Come on, Laddie," I said, tugging his leash. "I guess we'd better not take the time to drop him off at home."

"I doubt that Pamela will mind."

"I don't know. She may not appreciate it. She doesn't have any pets of her own, and she's only ever seen Laddie at some of our outdoor shows and then only for a few minutes."

"Nonsense! Pamela loves dogs. Rich was the one who didn't want any animals in the house."

"Oh, I didn't know that. Well, let's get on the road."

"I sure hope nothing's wrong," Susan said.

"Me, too."

In the few minutes it took us to reach Pamela's house, we tried to assure each other that chances were everything was all right, but we both felt a bit uneasy.

When we turned onto Pamela's street, my stomach knotted at the sight of an ambulance parked in the semi-circular driveway, next to the front door.

"Oh, no!" Susan said. "Oh, Pamela!"

Chapter 40

I parked well back from the ambulance so that my car wouldn't be in the way. As I turned off the engine, two paramedics, rolling somebody on a gurney, came out.

Susan clutched my arm, and we held our breaths.

"Can you see who it is?" I asked her.

"No. I can't tell. Wait a minute. Here comes Mrs. Bramble."

"Look! There's Pamela right behind her!"

Our friend had followed her housekeeper out of the house, and they were both standing on the sidewalk watching the paramedics load their patient into the ambulance.

We got out of the car, and I grabbed Laddie's leash as he jumped down from the back seat, onto the driveway. I held his leash firmly and kept him by my side as we rushed to Pamela, who appeared to be comforting her housekeeper.

"What happened?" Susan asked.

"It's John," Mrs. Bramble replied. "He came over to help me get some crystal down from the high shelves in the kitchen cabinets, and he suddenly got dizzy. Then he lost his balance and fell. I think he's hurt his back again, just when he was starting to feel better," she wailed. "It's all my fault! I never should have asked him to help."

"He hasn't had any dizzy spells before, has he?" Pamela asked.

"Well, no, he's never complained about being dizzy."

"Then there's no way you could have anticipated a problem. You can't blame yourself, Mary."

"I need to get to the hospital."

"Of course. I'll drive you."

"No, no. You have to deal with your business problems. I can drive myself."

I had to agree with Pamela that Mrs. Bramble was in no condition to drive herself anywhere. Her hands were shaking, and tears were running down her cheeks.

"I'll take you," Susan volunteered.

"OK," she agreed, "but we'll need to run by the park and pick up the kids from their tennis lessons on the way."

"Sure, we can do that."

Mrs. Bramble went back into the house and returned, carrying her purse and car keys, which she handed to Susan. We watched as they drove away. As soon as the Brambles' car was out of sight, Laddie began to pull at his leash again.

"Hey, Laddie," Pamela said softly, reaching down to stroke his soft fur.

"I'm glad you're here," she told me. "I was just about to call you when John hurt himself. "

"Dawn asked me to stop by. She was concerned because she hadn't heard from you. Dawn and Ralph both called several times this morning but couldn't get through."

"My fault. I should have let them know at the gallery that I couldn't come in this morning. I'll check in later."

"I'm texting her now to let them know."

"Thanks, Amanda. I appreciate it. Let's go inside now."

"Are you sure you want a dog in the house? I can walk him around to the patio."

"Yes, let's go out to the patio, but there's no need to take him around the side. Come on through."

"All right."

"Why did you think I wouldn't want Laddie in the house?"

"I didn't know, but since you don't have any pets, I thought maybe it wasn't a good idea."

"No, it's fine. Rich always said being around dogs or cats made him sneeze, so we didn't have any."

"I understand. Allergies can be hard to deal with."

"I'd love to adopt a dog, but, under the circumstances, the time certainly isn't right since I may not be here to take care of a dog," she added glumly.

"We haven't given up trying to find Rich's killer."

"I know, Amanda, and I appreciate everything you and Susan have done. Anyway, I have another crisis to deal with today. I wanted to talk to you about it because you're not involved in Rich's company, and you can give me an objective opinion."

As Pamela spoke, we moved inside, walking down the hall toward the kitchen and den.

"Don't let Laddie into the kitchen," Pamela cautioned. "I need to clean up the broken crystal in there. You can take him out to the patio through the den."

I did as Pamela suggested and waited for her on the patio. Since the backyard was enclosed, I unsnapped Laddie's leash and let him wander around. Unlike many retrievers, Laddie didn't fancy swimming and had refused all our past efforts to coax him to join us in the water whenever we visited any friends or relatives who had a pool. He walked around the edge of Pamela's pool but showed no interest in diving in.

"All taken care of," Pamela said when she joined me on the glider. "I was wondering why John didn't grab onto the countertop when he felt dizzy, but I found two broken wine glasses. I think he must have been holding one in each hand, and he probably didn't want to drop them because I know Mary would have warned him to be extra careful. In all the years she's worked for us, she's never broken so much as a saucer."

"I hope he's not badly injured."

"So do I. Mary's had a lot to deal with, considering all her family's health problems, and now my situation isn't helping, either."

"I'm sure Susan will call us from the hospital as soon as they're able to talk to the doctors."

"Yes, if his condition turns out to be serious, Mary will need to take some time off. I should have gone with her to the hospital, but I have to make a decision fairly soon about what to do with Rich's company. That's what Mary was talking about when she said I needed to deal with my business problems."

"Why the rush?"

"Something's come up. That's why I didn't go into the gallery this morning, but I'm kicking myself for not interrupting the Zoom meeting I was having with Sheila and Fred long enough to let Ralph know."

"He understands you have a lot on your plate."

"Even so, I should have called him. I was so rattled over this latest development that I forgot all about the Roadrunner. We had our lawyer and the accountant who's conducting the in-depth audit join the meeting for a while, too. Of course, they all had their own opinions, and I don't know what to do. Let me tell you about it and see what you think."

"OK, Pamela, but I'm no genius when it comes to business. I'm getting to know the art business a little better than I did when I first went full time, but that's about it."

"I think you've done very well, landing on your feet and being able to support yourself with your art. Anyway, I value your opinion. It seems that the embezzlement isn't our only problem. Our biggest client just declared bankruptcy, and it's Chapter 7, not Chapter 11."

My blank expression betrayed my ignorance of the terminology.

"They're going to liquidate, not reorganize. We'll probably never collect a dime and they owe us plenty. Added to the embezzlement, this client's bankruptcy is enough that we could get tipped into filing, too. Evidently, the company in California that had offered to buy us out a while back found out about it and withdrew their offer. Then they came back in with a low-ball offer. Their latest offer wouldn't do much more than get the company out from under our debt."

"Oh. So either bankruptcy or a buyout that won't net you much?"

"Yes. It's up to me to decide, of course. Either way, I'm going to take a huge financial hit unless Fred's right that we could pull off a reorganization, rather than a liquidation, but he's the only one in favor of that option."

"Is there some reason that Fred's pushing for—what is it?—Chapter 11?"

"Nothing very concrete. He's convinced that the sales staff have some good leads for new business. It's going to be a while before Fred's a hundred percent, and I don't know whether he's being overly optimistic or not."

"I think it's probably worth a shot. If you're going to lose everything anyway, what would it hurt?"

"Hmm. You make a good point. Sheila's pushing for selling, but I'm not thrilled about giving up Rich's company to these Silicon Valley sharks. They didn't waste any time cancelling their previous offer and coming back with a lower one. Plus, they're pushing hard for an immediate decision."

I'd put my bag down next to the glider earlier, and Laddie kept nosing around it while Pamela and I talked. He knew I kept a spare hard rubber ball in there, and he was probably in the mood for a game of fetch. I reached inside to grab his ball and heard my phone go off at the same time. I glanced at the display.

"It's Jennifer," I told Pamela before picking up.

She looked confused.

"I painted a pet portrait of her dog."

"Oh, right. Go ahead. I'll grab us some coffee."

With a frustrated Laddie looking on, I answered Jennifer.

"Just wanted to let you know I'm back in town. I had such a great time in San Jose, but it's a relief to be back on the ground. The flight back was terribly choppy. Next time Hal invites me to fly with him, I think I'll pass. It was that scary."

"Hal?"

"You know, Hal Quinlin. I told you we were friends."

"Of course. I didn't know he was a pilot."

"Yes, he has his own small plane, but I'm flying strictly commercial from now on. Anyway, I was wondering when I could come by to see Betsey's portrait."

"How about tomorrow evening? My studio's on Lonesome Valley's regular Friday night studio tour, so anytime between six and nine would be fine."

"Great! I'll stop by then. I can't wait to see it!"

"See you then."

Laddie had continued to nudge my bag during my brief conversation with Jennifer, and his eagerness to play fetch distracted me momentarily. As I reached for the ball, I realized that Jennifer had alerted me to another possible phony alibi. Perhaps Nate wasn't the only person to deliberately set up a fake one. I'd assumed that Hal had driven back to Lonesome Valley from Las Vegas the day that Rich was murdered, but he could have flown. If he'd piloted his own plane that day, he could easily have returned in time to stab Rich.

By this time, Laddie was bouncing around with anticipation, so I stood up and tossed the ball for him to chase, just as Pamela came out with our coffee. She set my mug down on a small table next to the glider and took a sip of her own coffee while we watched Laddie scramble for his ball and run back to me, dropping the ball at my feet, eager for more of his favorite game.

I picked it up and threw it again, but my aim was off, and it rolled under a dense bush against the side wall. Laddie poked around the bush with his nose, but when he didn't find his ball, he turned to me and gave a little yip.

"Oops! Do you have a broom I could use to fish around for his ball?"

"Sure," Pamela said, setting her mug down next to mine. "There's one in the pool house. I'll get it for you. I take it this isn't the first time a bush ate his ball."

"Afraid not. So far, we've lost two balls, so I always keep a spare, just in case."

Pamela laughed and went to find the broom while I headed to the bush and held the lower branches aside, hoping to spot Laddie's ball. When Pamela handed me the broom, I felt around underneath the bush with it, even though I couldn't see the end of the broom.

"I think I feel it," I said, pulling the broom back toward me. I reached under the bush. "I can't quite reach it."

Laddie crouched down and poked his nose back into the bush, but he couldn't get to the ball, either.

"Let me try," Pamela suggested, and I handed her the broom.

While she prodded the bush, Laddie right beside her, I stood up and massaged my neck, rotating it around to limber up.

That's when I spotted it.

On top of the wall, almost hidden behind the leafy bush, was a home-security-system camera and it was pointed toward Pamela's backyard.

Someone was watching every move we made!

Chapter 41

Gasping, I pointed to the camera.

"Someone's been keeping tabs on you and Rich."

"Hal?"

"It's his yard."

"I can't believe it! My neighbor's a voyeur."

"I'll bet he's more than that. I think he's a killer."

Pamela covered her mouth with her trembling hand. She looked as though she might pass out.

Laddie, still intent on finding his ball, had buried his head in the bush again.

"Well, hello, ladies."

Pamela was so startled at seeing Hal's head pop up a few feet away from us on the other side of the wall that she screamed, and Laddie immediately withdrew from the bush and leaned against her leg.

"Sorry, Pamela. I didn't mean to scare you, but I think you've got the wrong idea."

Before we could protest, Hal jumped up on the wall and dropped down into Pamela's backyard, just as he'd done the evening of the Fourth of July party when he'd confronted Rich about the fireworks he'd been setting off.

I was sure he'd heard every word we'd said. Otherwise, I doubted that he'd think that we had the wrong idea, as he put it.

He took a couple steps towards us, and we both backed up.

"Hey, there. No need to act that way. I'm harmless."

"I don't think so." As soon as the words were out of my mouth, I regretted saying them. He took another step forward, and Laddie's low growl erupted into a loud bark.

"Can't you shut that dog up?" he said to me. "I want to talk to Pamela."

"Well, I don't want to talk to you," she responded. "You belong in jail!"

"Whoa, there, little lady. My camera just got turned around somehow; that's all."

"All by itself? That doesn't seem very likely to me," I said.

"*You* stay out of this!" he yelled, eliciting more barking from Laddie.

"I don't want her to stay out of this," Pamela said, linking arms with me, "and I'd like you to leave right now."

"Not till we straighten this out. It's just a simple misunderstanding. I am *not* spying on you."

"Maybe not, but you *were* spying on Rich, weren't you?" I asked.

Pamela raised an eyebrow.

"If I don't miss my guess, he's the one behind the low-ball offer for Rich's company," I told Pamela, before addressing Hal. "You wanted to take over, and Rich wasn't going to sell. Is that why you killed him?"

"Now look. You have the wrong idea."

240

He started towards us again, and we retreated toward the pool. I was tempted to pull Pamela's arm and urge her to run, but Hal could have easily caught up with us in a matter of seconds.

"I only want to talk with you. Let me explain."

By this time we were standing next to the corner of the pool, and the patio door wasn't too far away, but if we ran for it, I didn't think we could make it inside and get the slider closed before he reached us.

"OK, why don't you do that," I said in an effort to buy time, as Laddie continued to growl at Hal, who glared at him before turning his attention back to Pamela.

"All right. Look. There's nothing wrong with my wanting to buy Rich's company. I'm a businessman. I do business."

"So you admit the offer's coming from your company? Some businessman. Spying on your neighbor. You should be ashamed of yourself."

Hal shrugged. "Whatever works. It's nothing personal."

"That's an outrageous statement, if I ever heard one," Pamela said.

"Especially since you stabbed Rich," I added. "Why did you do it? Was it because you overheard Rich talking about his decision to go public when you wanted his company for yourself? Did you think Pamela would be easier to deal with if Rich wasn't around?"

Hal's face contorted with anger and his voice dropped to almost a whisper. "I'll thank you to stop making unfounded accusations, or you could find yourselves on the wrong end of a libel suit."

"I don't think so. It's not libel if it's true!"

"You have absolutely no proof of that!" he snarled, starting towards us once again.

Laddie startled us all when he let out a string of loud, staccato barks before rushing toward Hal and nipping at his jeans. He raised his arm to hit Laddie, bringing it down quickly, but my golden boy was faster than Hal as he first darted out of the way and then came back and grabbed Hal's bootcut jeans in his mouth, giving them a hard tug. Hal took another swipe at Laddie but missed as my retriever ran between his legs, plunging into the pool. Hal lost his balance and fell in after him.

I ran toward the pool steps on the opposite side and called Laddie who swam toward me. Whether he liked the water or not, he was a natural swimmer. He scrambled out of the pool and shook himself, spraying water all over me before running back to the edge of the pool near where Hal was attempting to pull himself onto the deck. Pamela was discouraging him by tapping his hands with the broom we'd been using earlier to try to locate Laddie's ball. Hal kept grabbing for the broom, and Pamela kept swinging it out of his way, but I was afraid he'd eventually succeed in pulling her into the water and getting out himself.

Laddie wasn't about to tolerate Hal's shenanigans, though. He rushed over to help Pamela keep Hal at bay.

"I'm calling the police! Stay where you are!" I warned Hal.

"Get that dog away from me!" he yelled, but I ignored him and completed my call.

Every time Hal approached the edge of the pool, Laddie began snarling like a mad dog and barking ferociously. If I hadn't known that he was the friendliest dog in the world, I'd have been frightened of him myself.

I took Pamela's arm and gently tugged her back a few feet from the pool's edge while we watched Laddie guard Hal.

It was a long five minutes before Lieutenant Belmont and two patrol officers I'd never seen before arrived, and Pamela ran to the front door to let them in.

As they stepped out, onto the patio, Lieutenant Belmont took in the scene before him.

"Hmm. What's all this?"

He motioned to the patrol officers to get Hal out of the pool and called Laddie to him.

"Looks like you've been a busy boy. We'll take it from here." Laddie basked in the lieutenant's praise and didn't waste any time coming closer and rubbing his side against the lieutenant, leaving his pants leg with a big wet smear, but the lieutenant patted him, anyway.

Swatting away the extended hands of one of the cops, Hal hauled himself out of the pool and was promptly handcuffed.

"You can't do that!" he yelled. "I haven't done a thing."

I'd already shared my theory about Hal's crime with Lieutenant Belmont, but since there was no proof, I figured the lieutenant wouldn't be able to arrest Hal for Rich's murder, but he could arrest him for something else. He'd certainly threated Pamela and me. I had no doubt that Laddie's intervention had prevented Hal from doing us all violence, Laddie included.

"That's not what I hear," the lieutenant told him. "Read him his rights."

"I'll sue each and every one of you. I'm not a criminal. You have no proof that I killed Rich!"

"I don't recall mentioning anything about Mr. Smith's murder."
The lieutenant rubbed his chin. "You're under arrest for trespassing
and assault. . . for now."

"What do you mean 'for now'?"

I was wondering the same thing myself. Hal was right. We could
provide no proof that he'd stabbed Rich.

"I meant what I said," the lieutenant replied cryptically. "Take him
away."

"What am I going to do?" Pamela asked. "He'll be out on bond the
minute his lawyer arranges bail, and he lives right next door to me."

"Don't worry, Mrs. Smith. I have the feeling that you're not going
to have to deal with Mr. Quinlin anytime soon. I just got a report back
from the state lab. They found DNA on the knife and your husband's
shirt, and it wasn't yours."

Chapter 42

When she showed up at my studio the following evening to see Betsy's portrait, I didn't have the heart to tell Jennifer that her friend had been arrested. I knew she'd find out soon enough, but the bad news didn't need to come from me. I was pleased that she loved her beagle's picture and couldn't wait to hang it in her den.

It turned out to be a tense two weeks before the state lab made a DNA match with Hal. In the meantime, Lieutenant Belmont pulled out all the stops so that the district attorney would charge Hal with murder, and he wouldn't be able to get bail, as Pamela had done.

It didn't hurt that Chip admitted seeing Rich at the park with a knife. Evidently, Rich had purposely brought it to slash the painting Chip had given Pamela, but, ironically, it turned out to be the weapon that was used to kill him. Somehow, Hal had managed to get his hands on it and turn it against Rich.

The clincher was that a man came forward who had seen Rich arguing with Hal. The witness, an artist from Phoenix who was in town for Art in the Park, had packed his paintings up early and left for home without ever hearing about the murder. It was a pure luck that someone in his artists' guild mentioned the killing during their monthly meeting. Although he'd had no idea that what he'd seen had any significance at the time, his sighting proved that Hal had lied about his alibi.

The district attorney had refused to drop the charges against Pamela until the DNA match with Hal was confirmed. He never apologized for the mistake, though, which he blamed on police incompetence.

The D.A. also had taken a dim view of Nate's fabricated alibi, even though it turned out that Nate had been with his dispatcher, rather than the customer/girlfriend who had vouched for him at the time of the murder. Evidently, Nate had been trying to juggle two girlfriends, and his suggestion to them both to lie about his whereabouts was motivated by his fear that they would each find out about the other. His concerns were realized when they were all questioned about their stories, and he was left without any girlfriends, rather than two.

Pamela's anxiety about the possibility that Hal would be released on bail made her wary, but she felt relieved when bail was denied. His high-powered lawyers hadn't managed to convince the judge that Hal wasn't a flight risk. With his considerable resources and his own airplane at the ready, Hal very well could have left the court's jurisdiction.

At last, Pamela was able to have a memorial service for her husband and lay him to rest. Brian and I attended, along with all the members of the Roadrunner. Pamela sat in the front pew with some of her relatives, but it was Mrs. Bramble who held her hand and comforted her throughout the service, while her husband John sat behind them. He'd suffered a concussion when he'd fallen in Pamela's kitchen, but he'd since recovered.

Although Pamela didn't notice, I saw Lieutenant Belmont sitting in the back row during the service, but he slipped out before the minister intoned the benediction.

Everybody who worked at R. J. Smith Software was there to pay their respects, too, even Fred, who hadn't recovered from his accident, but who'd insisted on coming, anyway.

Despite his injuries that the police now suspected may have been caused by Cheri Logan's jealous former boyfriend, Fred had returned to work. Since there was little hope of locating Will, let alone convincing him to return the money he'd embezzled, and with the offer from Hal's company to do a buy-out off the table, Fred and Sheila were pushing the sales staff hard to produce new business. They'd had enough initial success, even though the situation remained touch and go, that he'd continued to encourage Pamela to hold off on declaring bankruptcy. In the meantime, she was leaving the rest of the money that Rich had used to replace the embezzled funds in the company's coffers to cover payroll and other expenses.

Things were slowly getting back to normal for me, too, now that Hal was in jail and Pamela had been exonerated, but I was well aware that Pamela's life had been turned upside down. There would be no getting back to normal for her, now that she'd lost Rich, and I knew it was going to be a daily struggle for her just to get by, even though she had the support of all her friends and Mrs. Bramble's constant solicitation.

Pamela was a trooper, though, and she was doing her best to keep busy. She didn't waste any time coming back to the gallery on her regular schedule, and she'd resumed painting, along with holding her open studio on Friday nights.

I was content that Belle and Dennis were back from their vacation, and Laddie perked up at the sight of his little buddy Mr. Big. Brian and I were back on track, and Emma and Matt's plans were going forward with less resistance from Ned, who'd finally decided that it was in his own best interest not to object to Emma's wishes.

Since Laddie had proved to be such an adept swimmer, Pamela had invited us over for him to take a dip in her pool, but he refused to go near it, even when I threw his ball—the one we'd finally recovered from under the bush—into the water. I gave up after my one attempt to coax him into the pool.

"You're definitely a landlubber, Laddie," I said.

"Woof!"

"We're lucky he wasn't a landlubber when we needed him most. Laddie's a good boy!" Pamela said, as she dangled a freeze-dried salmon treat in front of his nose.

He took it gently in his soft retriever's mouth and licked the crumbs from Pamela's hand after he'd swallowed the snack she'd given him.

"Woof! Woof!" he agreed.

Sparkling
Limeade

Amanda finds a glass of sparkling limeade refreshing during the summer. She admits to having a sweet tooth, so she always adds an extra teaspoon of sugar to her drink. It's easy to adjust the sweetness of your own limeade by increasing or decreasing the amount of sugar in this recipe.

Ingredients

juice of one lime (or 2 tablespoons)
2 tablespoons sugar
8 ounces ice-cold seltzer water
tiny pinch of salt
thin slice of lime for garnish (optional)

Directions

Chill a glass. Before juicing the lime, cut a thin slice for garnish, if desired. Combine lime juice, sugar, and salt in the glass and stir with an iced tea spoon until the sugar and salt are dissolved. Add the cold seltzer water a little at a time since the carbonation in it will cause foaming. Add garnish. Stir and enjoy!

Makes one serving.

Chicken Salad with Cranberries and Grapes

Whenever Amanda wants a quick and tasty sandwich without having to turn on the oven or fire up the burners, she whips up some chicken salad. This is the same recipe she used when she took chicken salad sandwiches along for a "picnic" when she staked out the Brambles' house with Susan, who said she absolutely loved it!

Ingredients

12.5-ounce can of cooked chicken breast, chunk style, in water, drained

⅓ cup mayonnaise

½ cup sweetened, dried cranberries

½ cup seedless grapes, halved

¼ cup chopped pecans

1 tablespoon green onion, minced

2 teaspoons lime juice

⅛ teaspoon salt

⅛ teaspoon pepper

Directions

Drain chicken and cut large chunks into smaller ones if necessary. Mince the green onion. Cut the grapes in half. Combine chicken and mayonnaise. Add cranberries, grapes, pecans, green onion, lime juice, salt, and pepper and stir well. Refrigerate any chicken salad that you don't use right away. Store in refrigerator for up to two days.

Makes four servings.

Salmon Salad for Two

Amanda likes to prepare this salad when she and Emma are dining alone because it's one of Emma's favorites.

Ingredients

8 ounces salmon
1 tablespoon olive oil
½ teaspoon salt
dash fresh ground pepper
2 cups mixed greens
1 peach, chopped
½ cup raspberries
raspberry vinaigrette salad dressing

Directions

Remove skin from salmon, cut it in strips, and season it with salt and pepper. Heat olive oil in a skillet on medium-high heat. Add the salmon, and sear for about four minutes, until crisp. Do not move the salmon during grilling. Turn the salmon over and continue grilling about five minutes until done. Turn off the heat and set the skillet aside while assembling the salad. Add one cup of salad greens to each of two individual salad bowls. Arrange the salmon strips on top. Chop a peach, and add half on top of the salmon in each bowl. Sprinkle half of the raspberries over the salad in each bowl. Dress to taste with raspberry vinaigrette salad dressing.

Makes two servings.

Rhubarb Jam
Coffee Cake

Amanda knows she won't have to wait until rhubarb is in season to savor the flavor because she can bake her favorite coffee cake using rhubarb jam. Luckily for Amanda, her cousin keeps her well supplied because she grows rhubarb and makes her own jam, which she's always happy to send to her favorite cousin.

Topping Ingredients

½ cup brown sugar, packed
2 tablespoons all-purpose baking mix
½ teaspoon cinnamon
2 tablespoons cold butter
⅓ cup chopped pecans

Cake Ingredients

2 cups all-purpose baking mix
⅔ cup milk
1 egg
⅓ cup mayonnaise
2 tablespoons sugar
½ teaspoon cinnamon
½ cup rhubarb jam

Directions

Preheat the oven to 350 degrees. In a small mixing bowl, combine sugar, baking mix, and cinnamon. Cut in butter with a fork until the mixture looks pebbly. Add the pecans and stir. Set aside. In a larger mixing bowl, combine milk, egg, mayonnaise, sugar, and cinnamon. Add the baking mix and stir well. In a buttered eight- or nine-inch round cake pan, spread two-thirds of the cake batter. Add the rhubarb jam to the top of the cake batter by small spoonfuls, covering as much of the batter as possible. Cover with the remaining third of the cake batter. Sprinkle the topping as evenly as possible over the cake batter. Bake for thirty minutes at 350 degrees. Remove the coffee cake from the oven and place it on a cooling rack. If you're serving it warm, ten to fifteen minutes should be enough cooling. Store any coffee cake that you don't use right away in an air-tight container. Stored coffee cake can be reheated in the microwave, if you wish.

Makes eight servings.

About the Author

USA Today bestselling author Paula Darnell is a former college instructor who has a Bachelor of Arts in English degree from the University of Iowa and a Master of Arts in English degree from the University of Nevada, Reno. *Killer Art in the Park* is the fourth book in her Fine Art Mystery series. She's also the author of the DIY Diva Mystery series and *The Six-Week Solution*, a historical mystery set in Reno. She resides in Las Vegas with her husband Gary and their golden retriever Lindsey Lou.

VISIT HER WEBSITE

pauladarnellauthor.com

Books by Paula Darnell

DIY Diva Mystery Series

Death by Association

Death by Design

Death by Proxy

Fine Art Mystery Series

Artistic License to Kill

Vanished into Plein Air

Hemlock for the Holidays

Killer Art in the Park

Historical Mystery

The Six-Week Solution